I0739635

DREAMSTALKER

A Dreamstrider Novel

By

C. E. CZERNIEJEWSKI

This is a work of fiction. Names, characters, places, and events are either the product of the author's imagination or are used fictitiously. Any resemblance at actual persons, living or dead, events, or locales is entirely coincidental.

Acknowledgements

What you are reading is the result of several years of work and could not have happened without the help of others.

Thank you to my early readers and the members of my writing group for your feedback and encouragement. Thank you to Roberta and Greg Parrott for sharing their medical knowledge and providing information about the procedures followed by first responders - any lack of authenticity or errors are entirely my fault. Thank you to my copyeditor, Ashley Mason, for tightening my prose, and to Dane Low for a cover that far exceeds my imaginings. And, finally, to my family, thank you for your support and blind faith in my abilities.

For my sons and daughter

CHAPTER ONE

THE UNSPOKEN CALLING of her name woke her. With a yawn Lindsey stretched, arching her back and reaching over her head. Her fingers splayed then curled with knuckle-cracking force. Her body relaxed onto a hard, uneven surface, and she blinked blurry eyes at the unexpected sensation. She ran a hand over her face, rubbing the tips of her fingers across one eye then the other in an attempt to speed her waking. At the cool brush of grass against her arm as she lowered it, she rolled her head to the side and stared without comprehension. For a few heartbeats, she studied the stiff stems and supple blades that arose before her.

Where am I? The confused inquiry held no fear. Turning her head, she saw a vibrant blue sky peeking at her through the gentle swaying of the grass. She sat up, planting her hands behind her.

The shoulder-high grass, interspersed with delicate wildflowers of pale purple, spread out in an undulating sea, flowing down the hill upon which she sat. Mountains rose in the distance. Their jagged profiles and snow-capped peaks contrasted sharply against the azure sky. A quick look showed that the mountain chain formed a continuous ring around her, yet the air carried the soothing sound of ocean waves. Lindsey wrinkled her brow at the incongruity.

She climbed to her feet, wiping her hands on her denim-clad thighs. The breeze played around her, tugged at her hair, and murmured of the sea. She turned slowly, seeking the promised body of water, and the breeze followed. Always, it kissed her face and never struck from behind. The ocean it spoke of was nowhere to be seen.

The movement of the grass caught Lindsey's eye. Its soft rustling sounded distinct from the ebb and flow of the tide, but the movement synchronized with that of the invisible sea. Closing her eyes, she immersed herself in the tale the wind told. She felt waves wash through her before withdrawing, only to return again, the rocking of an ancient lullaby luring her back to sleep.

She swayed, and her eyes snapped open. The sight that greeted her caused her breath to catch; the scattered wildflowers had multiplied and now stretched far around her, a multicolored blanket of reds, yellows, white, and purples. Kneeling down among the tiny blossoms, she cupped one of the delicate blooms and stroked its silken petals. She inhaled deeply but, despite being surrounded by flowers, detected no fragrance on the breeze, the only flaw in an otherwise perfect dream.

She stilled as realization settled over her. She surveyed her surroundings through narrowed eyes, and a sense of familiarity took root as she recognized the hill as one of those nonsensical places she had once regularly visited during her nighttime wanderings. Dropping her chin to her chest, she smiled and shook her head, feeling foolish for not recognizing the dream for what it was sooner.

She sat down and leaned back, bracing herself on her elbows. The flowers and grass wove in and out of her vision as she gazed at the clear blue sky. She sighed in appreciation of the peace and calm and welcomed the respite from the real world and its demands, even if the respite was within her own head and of her own imagining.

A bud bumped her cheek. The wind caught it and blew it against her skin again. She reached up to rid herself of the tickling sensation, her hand stopping halfway as a wisp of cloud appeared in the sky. Even as she watched, a patch of blue faded then billowed into white fluff. A frisson of unease worked across her scalp and slid down her spine. Sitting up straight, Lindsey scanned the sky. Stray clouds dotted the horizon. She bit her lower lip and furrowed her brow.

The wind changed direction, gusting from behind her and whipping her hair into her face. She shivered. Then she felt a presence behind her, a bright light in her mind's eye that inexorably drew her. She closed her eyes with recognition.

He was here.

Lindsey brought her knees to her chest and wrapped her arms around them. She dug her toes into the damp soil. Willing the forming tears not to fall, she stared straight ahead and drew in a shuddering breath. "I thought you were dead."

As he drew near, the flowers receded and the grass shrank to half its original height, leaving the two of them exposed atop the hill within a circle of depressed foliage. He said nothing, stepped to her right, and sank down next to her.

Out of the corner of her eye, she watched him as he balanced on the balls of his sneaker-clad feet. His elbows rested on his knees. He plucked a piece of grass and began to toy with it, running it through his fingers, rolling, twisting, and knotting it. He threw it to the ground with a sharp stabbing motion. "I'm sorry."

She looked down at her feet and tucked an auburn lock behind her left ear, frustrated at the lack of explanation for where he had been for the past four years. Lindsey tried to turn and demand an answer, but her body suddenly felt leaden, like in one of those dreams where she was stuck on train tracks. The harder she tried to move, the more her body resisted. In the many years she had known him, only once had she been able to see him clearly. Resigned that she would once more be unable to look directly at him, she rested her forehead on her knees. He sighed and said, "I have something for you. I'm not sure you're going to want it, but I'm fairly certain you're going to need it."

Lindsey heard him moving. She sensed rather than saw him stand and move in front of her.

"Here."

She slowly lifted her head and raised her eyes. He was an indistinct blur as he knelt on one knee before her, but what he held out to her was perfectly clear: a sword.

Like a knight offering his sword to his liege, he held the hilt over his forearm with the sheathed blade gripped in his other hand. Yet the sword was hers, not his. She knew the weight of it. The slender elegance hidden inside the hardened leather. The strength of the blade itself. It seemed to shine before her, putting her idyllic surroundings in gloom. She could not look away from it, and her hand rose of its own volition to reclaim it.

With a sharp intake of breath she stopped short of taking the sword. Her hand dropped, fisted into her lap. She turned her head away from him and swallowed hard. "No. It's not mine. Not anymore," she said. "I no longer walk those paths." The words came from somewhere deep within. She could only guess their meaning, but they felt right. They felt true.

"That's not entirely true, Lindsey, is it? You're here now. And it's not the first time since—" When she still made no move to take the sword, he laid the blade in the grass before her. "I know this isn't what you want. I'm sorry. But you may not have a choice."

She felt his hand cover hers. The jolt of awareness at the contact overshadowed the lure of the sword, and she felt the hum of the connection they had always shared. She turned her hand so their palms touched and their fingers interlaced. *I've missed you.*

As if he had heard the thought, he gave her hand a light squeeze. Then, after a quick caress with his thumb, he withdrew his hand. He stood and was gone.

Lindsey gasped at his abrupt departure.

Damn. She cursed herself for not finding some way to keep him with her.

She turned her attention to the sword. Tentatively, she reached out to it and ran her fingertips down its covered length. She grasped the hilt in her right hand and the sheath in her left. Slowly, she drew the sword out. The double-edged steel gleamed with an aching familiarity. Memories long laid to rest stirred.

The sudden rumble of thunder startled her, and she looked to the horizon. Storm clouds gathered over the distant peaks, dark billowing masses roiling in. Her grip on the sword tightened as alarm wove its way through her. This was her space. Clouds had no place here; a storm had even less. Something was wrong.

An unfamiliar sound and a hint of movement came from behind her. For a brief moment she hoped he had come back, but the hope died quickly. She would recognize him anywhere, and the presence behind her was not his golden warmth but the cold, shiny darkness of obsidian. Malevolence and rage emanated from the trespasser.

Lindsey tried to get to her feet and turn to face the intruder. She tried to raise the blade to defend herself. Before her efforts came to fruition, she felt a searing pain penetrating between her shoulder blades through her chest.

Her breath came shallow and ragged. Excruciating. The metallic tang of blood filled her mouth. She looked down to see steel emerging from just below her sternum, continuing to come forward until she felt a body pressed against her back.

A hand grasped her shoulder.

"Welcome back, Lindsey," a voice purred in her ear. "I've been watching for you."

With a violent jerk the blade was yanked from her body. Blood poured from the wound, and she fell forward into the now-slick grass. Cold permeated her body; her vision became unfocused. Darkness claimed then released her as she woke, sweat-soaked, panting, and in pain.

CHAPTER TWO

LINDSEY OPENED HER eyes, not knowing where she was and not really caring. The throbbing pain in her abdomen and chest was all that mattered. Fearfully, she lifted a trembling hand to her stomach, fully expecting to feel blood. She closed her eyes in relief when she felt only the buttons and crisp cotton-poly blend of her blouse. She slowly straightened from her hunched-over position and ran her hands over her face.

She looked around at the rows of bookshelves and remembered where she was. *The library.* Her eight o'clock tutoring appointment had canceled at the last minute. She had decided to take advantage of the time to study for her own classes and had fallen asleep.

Looking down, she saw the corner of one

of her notebooks hanging over the edge of the desk. That would explain the pain in her stomach. The pain in her back had to be from too many naps at a desk and not enough sleep in her bed.

Pulling her cell phone out of her jacket pocket, she checked the time. It was nearly eleven. The library would be closing soon.

Moving awkwardly, she closed her books and notebooks and gathered them into a pile. She reached down for her backpack, but it was too far under the desk. Placing her hands on the edge of the desk, she pushed back the chair. She hooked the bag with her foot and pulled it toward her. She grabbed it then stood, grimacing at the lingering pain. She was fumbling with the bag's zipper pull when she felt someone give her waist a double-handed squeeze.

"Gotcha!"

With a startled shriek Lindsey jumped and twisted toward the voice. The movement knocked her off balance, and she fell heavily against the desk, knocking her books askew. She recognized the culprit as he reached out to steady her. His expression wavered between mischief and contrition.

"Jason Bradley, don't do that to me."

"Sorry." His lips twitched.

She rolled her eyes at him then turned around and started putting her things into the backpack. She looked up at Jason as she grabbed a notebook. "Why haven't you gone home yet?"

"I could ask the same of you." He handed her a pen.

She looked at the pen blankly.

"It was on the floor."

She shrugged, took it, and put it in with everything else then zipped the backpack closed.

He grabbed her jacket off the back of the chair and held it for her as she slid her arms into the sleeves. "I was over in the chem lab. Charles needed the night off," he explained as they walked to the elevator. "Then I went to the office. The intro class had a test today. I've been grading papers for the past four hours."

"What a way to spend a Friday night," Lindsey said.

"You're one to talk. I don't suppose your eight o'clock showed up?"

"No."

He sighed dramatically and shook his head. "Lindsey, Lindsey, Lindsey, when are you going to learn. No one wants to be here on a Friday night. The university knows this. That's why they close early on Fridays."

Lindsey shot him a look as they got on the

elevator. "Yeah, well, I needed to get some studying done anyway."

The doors closed and Jason pushed the button for the main level. "By the way, Makayla found me."

Lindsey fought a smile. "I'm sorry."

He shrugged. "She offered me a ride, and I mentioned you were probably here and suggested we check."

"I'm sure she loved that."

"Lindsey, she's a nice enough girl, but..."

Lindsey hooked elbows with him and gave his arm an affectionate squeeze. She finished for him, "She's just not for you. I've tried to tell her, but she thinks I want you for myself."

He smiled, and they rode the rest of the way in companionable silence.

They found Makayla waiting for them at the circulation desk. The petite brunette's eyes narrowed when she saw their linked arms. With a sigh Lindsey let go of Jason's arm. From the look he gave her, Lindsey knew he understood why she had done so. She was tired of dealing with her best friend's unrequited interest in Jason, her surrogate big brother. It made her feel awkward and unusually aware of him as an attractive member of the opposite sex.

"Hi, Makayla," Lindsey greeted her friend.

"Thanks for stopping for me."

"No problem," Makayla replied with a smile, though her eyes were on Jason.

The three of them left the library and started across campus to the parking lot. Ignoring the looks Jason shot her over his shoulder, Lindsey trailed behind the other two. As they passed other people, she found herself studying every man, hoping for a flicker of recognition, hoping to find the man from her dream now that she knew he was still alive.

They reached the parking lot and climbed into Makayla's car. Lindsey took the backseat, angling her legs to the side so Jason could push his seat further back. She tipped her head against the window and stared out unseeing as Makayla drove, smoothly shifting gears and whipping the car in and out of pools of streetlight.

Lindsey let her mind drift back to the dream and tried to recapture the details. He had told her she might need the sword. He had been right. Too bad she seemed to lack the skill to use it. She wondered if she had ever had the skill. Maybe she was simply out of practice. All of this was secondary to the real questions she wanted answered. Where had he been? Why had he waited until now to come to her?

"Lindsey?"

Lindsey looked up from her musings and realized they had stopped. Jason was already out of the car, leaning in and looking at her with amusement. "We're here."

"Sorry," she apologized. She turned to Makayla. "Thanks for the ride. We're still doing lunch Monday?"

Makayla grinned at her. "You know it. It's your turn to buy."

"I'll see you then." Bag in hand, Lindsey slid out of the car.

Jason leaned into the car again after she had gotten out and spoke to Makayla. "Thanks again. I'll walk from here."

"Are you sure?" Makayla asked, her disappointment obvious.

"Yeah. Have a good night." Jason straightened, closed the door, and stepped to Lindsey's side. Together they watched Makayla pull away and disappear down the street.

A crisp autumn breeze blew, setting the fallen leaves to rattle and rustle through yards and across the pavement. Out of the corner of her eye, Lindsey saw a shadow, and shivered and startled.

Jason took her hand and gave it a gentle tug, drawing her attention. "Are you okay? You seem kind of quiet tonight."

"I'm fine." She lifted a shoulder in a partial shrug. "I fell asleep in the library. Had a bad dream. It was, well, bad." With her free hand, she rubbed where the sword had pierced her. "And very vivid," she muttered.

He studied her. "Not a going-to-class-naked kind of dream, I take it."

"No." She gave him a weak smile. "A being-run-through-with-a-sword kind of dream."

"Ouch."

"Yeah."

"Do you want me to come in? I can hang here for a while if you want."

"No," she said with a slight shake of her head. "I'll be fine, but thanks for offering."

He nodded, not looking as if he believed her but accepting her answer. "If you're sure, I'll catch you later then." He leaned in, kissed her cheek, and gave her hand a quick squeeze before releasing it. He then turned and headed up the street toward his apartment, only two blocks away.

Rummaging through her pocket for her key, she walked the path and took the two steps to her front door. She unlocked and opened it. Hitting the light switch, she stepped inside, turning as she went, her eyes sweeping the area. Leaves flew. The trees swayed, and the wind sounded like a banshee's cry as it blew through the bare limbs. Lindsey shuddered. She closed and quickly bolted the door behind her.

She walked down the entrance hall to the kitchen. Shoving a pile of mail to the side, she set her bag on the counter. The red light blinked on the answering machine. She pressed the play button then hit "erase" when a prerecorded message about an upcoming bond issue started.

Kicking off her shoes and dropping her jacket on the chair at the entrance to the small living room, Lindsey turned on a lamp and walked over to the tall bookcase. A fishbowl with a lone goldfish sat on the second shelf just at eye level. She grabbed the canister of fish food next to the bowl and sprinkled a pinch into the water. As she watched the fish move to the surface to eat, she noted how cloudy the water was and felt a twinge of guilt.

"I'll clean your bowl in the morning," she promised.

Grabbing the television remote, she turned on the set and changed the channel for the last few minutes of the news. She returned to the kitchen, switched on the light, and rummaged through the freezer, selecting a fettuccine Alfredo entrée to microwave. With dinner started, she headed for her room at the end of the hall, looking forward to getting into her pajamas. She hoped the dull, throbbing ache in her back would go away once she was out of her bra. Entering her room, she reached for the lamp on the dresser next to the door. She turned on the lamp and glanced back down the hallway.

The whole apartment was brightly lit, she realized with surprise. Had she turned on every light in the place? When was the last time she had felt that compulsive need?

Probably close to four years now. Her mouth twisted with the sour thought. She quickly walked back the way she had come, hitting switches and turning off the lamp in the living room.

When she came to the floor lamp next to the sofa, she stared at it in consternation. She had no memory of turning it on, yet it shone, gently illuminating the small area. Standing in its light, the rest of the apartment suddenly seemed unbearably dark and left her feeling edgy. Calling herself childish for being spooked by the dark, she returned to her room.

Standing near her queen-size bed, Lindsey unbuttoned her blouse and shrugged out of it, wincing at the pain in her back. She undid her jeans and stepped out of them. The skin on her back stretched uncomfortably as she bent to remove her socks, and the dull ache in her abdomen intensified. As she reached behind to undo her bra, she saw a shadow out of the corner of her eye. Startled, she whirled and faced her image in the mirror. With a shaky laugh she scolded herself. *You've got to get a grip.* Then she froze and caught her breath at the sight of something just below her sternum.

Lindsey dashed to the bathroom, slapped on the light, and stared at the ugly bruise. Her fingers hovered over the mark. Touching it would make it real. She shook her head back and forth.

"No," she breathed. "No, no, *no!*" She met her gaze in the mirror. Pale and panicked, she bolted out of the bathroom to the kitchen, unmindful of the chilly air on her exposed body.

Grabbing her backpack, she yanked out her purse and upended it, spilling the contents on the counter. She pushed things this way and that, knocking stuff onto the floor until she found her compact. Clutching it, Lindsey ran back to the bathroom.

Turning her back to the mirror, she pulled her hair forward off her back. It took more than one try to open the compact. Then, with shaking hands, she lifted it and aimed the small mirror over her shoulder. At the sight of the dark purple mark, she whimpered. She turned to face the mirror again. For a moment, a ghostly afterimage of the sword protruding from her body hung before her eyes. She leaned against the wall and slowly slid down to the cold linoleum.

This can't be happening.

The words ran through her head in a loop. She had had more violent dreams than she could count. As a child she had woken nightly, filled with fear, afraid to move, and hugging a stuffed animal with each arm. She had been stabbed then, too. The pain had sometimes lingered when she was awake, but there had never been a mark the next day. Never. What had changed?

It had been years since she had had a dream like the one at the library. What was it she had told him? She no longer walked those paths. Exactly what those paths were, she could not say, but if it meant a return to nightly terror, she certainly wanted nothing to do with them.

Shivering, she got to her feet. Absently dropping the compact onto the bathroom counter, she walked to the dresser. She pulled out her favorite pajamas and crawled into them. The soft, worn cotton provided some measure of comfort.

Turning the lights on as she went, Lindsey

checked that every window was locked and that every blind was drawn. She double-checked that the front door was locked, trying not to think about how futile all her precautions were. What she feared could not be stopped by light or locks.

In the kitchen she took her now-lukewarm dinner out of the microwave, gave the pasta a quick stir, and set it to reheat for a minute. Her hand drifted to her midriff while she waited. Her thoughts turned back to the dream despite her efforts to think about something else, anything else.

I don't want to do this again, Lindsey protested in silent desperation.

You may no longer have a choice. His words echoed through her mind.

Lindsey jumped at the microwave's sharp beep. She pulled her food out and carried it to the living room. Folding her legs under her, she sank onto the couch and pulled her orange afghan down from the back of it. Wrapped in the afghan, she ate without tasting her food and stared unseeing at the television, dreading the inevitable, dreading falling asleep.

CHAPTER THREE

LINDSEY STOOD IN the middle of a dark parking lot with buildings on all sides. The buildings were awash in a silver-blue light as if there were a full moon, but when she looked up, there was nothing there. No moon. No stars. No sky. Just a grey expanse.

The buildings looked familiar. She felt like she had been here before. Or someplace like it. Tilting her head to the side, she looked at the building ahead of her. Was that her elementary school?

She took a step toward it to get a better look and the building changed shape, now looking like the old Shop and Save where her mother used to buy groceries.

Lindsey backed up a step.

The building remained unchanged.

She stepped forward again.

The shape of the building remained unaltered, but the light dimmed and the shadows lengthened.

Shivering in an unfelt breeze, Lindsey turned in place. There were no cars or any other people in the lot. She appeared to be alone, but she felt threatened. She hugged herself and debated what to do. She ruled out seeking shelter in one of the buildings. They were surrounded by growing pools of darkness that no light penetrated, and the sense of hostility in the air grew apace.

She eyed a path between two buildings. Light still shimmered along it. With one more glance around, she moved toward the path. As she stepped on it, she felt a sense of warmth and security. She knew with inexplicable certainty that if she could reach the other end of the path, she would be safe.

Traveling down it at a near jog, Lindsey tried to focus on the sparkling asphalt. She struggled to ignore the deep shadows to either side that seemed to pulse with ill intent.

From the corner of her eye she saw what seemed to be a massive shape looming toward her. Reflexively she glanced over, taking her eyes off the path.

Her right foot caught on something, causing her to lose her balance. She landed hard on her left foot and twisted it. She fell forward, just barely getting her hands out in front of her before crashing onto the sharp gravel. She hissed as the gravel bit into her hands and knees. Then she froze and stared down between her hands. Gravel. When had the path changed?

Gingerly, she shifted around to sit on the path. She turned her head to look back at the way she had come. Her breath caught in her throat. Gravel stretched behind her as far as she could see.

I'm on the wrong path. I must have made a wrong turn. How do you make a wrong turn on a straight path? She slapped a hand over her mouth to keep the rising hysteria from bubbling out. *I have to get out of here.*

Lindsey carefully got to her feet. She cautiously put her weight on her left foot and bit her lip at the pain. Seeing no other option, with nothing but the path before and behind her and darkness on either side, she limped forward.

Again she saw dark forms in her peripheral vision, but this time she kept her eyes on the path, determined to ignore the phantoms. But the shapes seemed to get more solid, more defined. Then she heard the crunch of gravel behind her. She hesitated and then continued to hobble along the path. The crunching followed her, kept pace with her. She stopped. Taking a deep breath, she looked behind her.

She was no longer alone. A great hulking shape stood there. His features were indistinct and cloaked in shadow, except for the gleam of his teeth as he grinned.

"Well, look what we've got," he growled.

A hard knot formed in Lindsey's stomach. Not wanting to take her eyes off him, but needing to know if he was talking to someone or was one of those people who spoke about themselves in the third person, she turned away from him. Seeing a second figure on the path before her, Lindsey nearly cried. A small moan did escape her when she realized the path had changed again. It was now dirt and pine needles, and woodlands replaced the darkness on either side.

"What do you think we ought to do with her?" asked the man behind her.

The man in front of her leered. "I can think of a few things." Making kissing noises, he held out a hand and wiggled his fingers. "Come on, kitten. Come here and let's have some fun."

The first man chortled.

Lindsey turned, putting her back to the woods, and looked back and forth between the two men. Both were huge. If either got ahold of her, she would be helpless.

Taking his lead from the second man, the first softly chanted, "Here, kitty, kitty. I have something I think you'll like."

Lindsey stepped back toward the woods, taking one cautious step after another. The men matched her step for step, slowly closing the distance between them.

She felt a subtle difference underfoot and shot a quick glance down. She was off the path. She clumsily pivoted and fled into the woods. She ran as fast as her throbbing ankle would let her, and, though her feet felt heavy, she crossed the ground with surprising smoothness.

The men crashed through the underbrush, whooping and calling out taunts as they pursued her.

Her breathing grew labored. The back of her throat felt raw and her lungs ached. She had a stitch in her side. She knew her pace had slowed, yet her pursuers seemed no closer. Instead of relief, she felt trepidation.

They're toying with me. Or herding me, she thought as she ran into a meadow with a log cabin sitting in the middle of it. *Into a trap.* She pulled up short as she finished the thought.

Bent over with a hand pressed to her side,

Lindsey studied the cabin. A simple log structure that looked like something on a bottle of syrup, the cabin seemed benign enough. Flowers grew along the foundation; calico curtains hung in the windows. There was even a lazy curl of smoke coming from the chimney. Why was she hesitating?

The sounds of the men's pursuit grew louder.

Feeling out of time, she slowly straightened and started for the front door. She prayed with every painful step that the door would be unlocked.

Behind her the men's voices grew louder. Their triumphant yells told her they had spotted her. The pounding of their footfalls sounded like thunder and seemed to shake the ground.

She reached the door, grabbed the handle, and pushed. The hinges squealed, but the door swung open. Without missing a step she crossed the threshold. Wobbling as she turned on her swollen ankle, she slammed the door shut.

She reached for a lock but found only two metal brackets attached to either side of the doorframe. Lindsey looked at them in rising panic. Then she spied a two-by-four in the corner. She grabbed it. Her hands shook as she dropped the board into the brackets, hoping the crossbeam would hold against the two men.

With all her attention focused on the door, she slowly backed away from it. She cringed in anticipation of the pounding that was sure to start any moment. Her breathing returned to normal, and still the men had not appeared.

She crept toward the window next to the door. With trembling fingers she pushed aside the curtain and looked outside. There was nothing but darkness, as if the windows had been painted black. Lindsey dropped the curtain and turned to survey her surroundings. They reminded her of an Andrew Wyeth painting.

The cabin consisted of a single room. There was a window on the wall to her left. From where she stood it looked every bit as black as the one by the door, yet sunlight filled the room and touched everything with a muted glow. Sparkling dust particles hung suspended in the air. A cast-iron potbelly stove sat in a corner, a wooden rocking chair next to it. A faded quilt in blue and white hung over the back of the chair. The floors were old wood, dulled with age.

Lindsey walked to the rocker and ran her hand over the quilt.

"Do you like it?" asked a smooth, deep voice. "It was my grandmother's."

Lindsey's hand fell to her side. She desperately wanted to turn and face the speaker but stood frozen in place. It felt as though a great weight had settled on her and a buzzing filled her ears.

The floor creaked as he moved up behind her.

"I'm impressed, Lindsey." He touched her right shoulder and trailed his fingers toward her spine. "Most wouldn't have been back after what I did to you." He traced down her spine to where he had stabbed her. "Still tender?" he inquired, his breath hot on her neck. Then he pressed on the bruise, and it took everything Lindsey had not to cry out at the pain.

He removed his hand, and Lindsey heard a blade being unsheathed. She struggled to move. The buzzing grew louder the harder she fought.

He snaked his left arm around her waist and pressed up against her. At the feel of the hard planes of his body and the corded strength in his arm, Lindsey felt a terrible vulnerability. When he brought his other arm around her, enclosing her in an obscene embrace, she saw the dagger he held. It gleamed in the sunlight. She closed her eyes and stopped struggling, waiting for him to stab her again and end the nightmare.

The buzzing faded and ceased.

The silence filled her with hope.

She slowly curled her toes.

No buzzing. No weight pressing down.

She opened her eyes.

"Let's see just how resilient you are," he purred, his lips brushing her ear. He brought the dagger to her neck.

She moved by instinct, raising her left hand to push against his right to keep the blade away from her throat. With her right hand, she reached up and pinched the underside of his arm as hard as she could while stomping on his toe.

He grunted and jerked the dagger away from her throat. The arm around her waist loosened. She twisted low under his right arm, driving her elbow into his ribs as she went around him. She started for the door.

The simple handle and crossbeam were gone, replaced by a knob. She reached for it. It started to turn before she grasped it. With a chill she remembered the men outside.

Taking a step away from the door, she turned to the man as he laughed, a deep throaty sound. Her eyes darted between him and the door as she retreated and put herself on the opposite side of the cabin from him. He was backlit, his features in shadow, but his pleasure at her predicament rolled off him in waves. She suspected her fear and desperation were as obvious to him.

"Come here, Lindsey." He gestured with the dagger. "Let's keep this between us. Come here, and I'll end this quickly. Otherwise..." He nodded toward the door that was slowly opening. "I'll let them have you."

She shook her head. No.

"You might want to reconsider, Lindsey." His voice became hard. "I can keep you here. I can keep you from waking. I can hold you in this place for as long as I want."

Of course. It's a dream, she thought. *Dreams can be changed. But how? Think, think, think. Oh God.*

One of the men who had chased her here stepped through the door. Grinning at her, he eased it shut behind him. "Nowhere to go, kitten."

I've got to get out of here.

She looked away from the men long enough to scan the room once more, hoping she had missed another exit. Nothing.

Her heart pounded a frantic beat. Rising panic choked her. Her vision became oddly blurred, with everything rippling in transparent waves like heat rising from pavement. She squeezed her eyes tight and opened them.

The ripples were still there.

She backed into the wall and gave a startled yelp at the motion against her back. Stepping away again, she saw that the wall was fluid, moving with the waves. There was nothing wrong with her vision. *The room was changing.*

Lindsey watched as the stove and rocker faded. A railing and stairs leading down appeared in their place as the waves stopped. She started edging around the room, hoping to get a straighter shot at the stairs, but how she was going to get past both men was beyond her.

"Get her," barked the man with the knife.

The other surged forward at his command, arms stretched before him. "You're mine now, kitten."

Lindsey felt a surge of anger. "I'm no one's kitten."

Without conscious thought, she launched herself at the man. An aura of soft white light seemed to form around her as she raced toward him. She felt the push-pull of the ocean tide. Her opponent seemed to get taller, but she was beyond caring.

The distance between them closed.

Growling, she leapt at him. Front paws of tawny gold struck him in the chest. Powerful back paws struck next. Her claws dug in and

left furrows across his chest as she pushed off
in the direction of the stairs, her tail moving
in counterbalance. She landed lightly. Sinew
moved smoothly under a sleek hide as her legs
alternately gathered and stretched, bringing her
closer to her goal. A knife struck the boards in
front of her, lodging in the wood with a solid
thunk. She bounded over it with easy grace.

When she reached the top of the stairs, she
leapt out into open space. Light once more engulfed her and her form blurred. Fur became
feathers. Paws became wings and talons. With
a cry of triumph she soared then folded her
wings along her sides and dove into the darkness below. At the last moment she tented her
wings and floated around the small space.

No doors.

No windows.

She circled back to the stairs.

A glimmer of light caught her eye. Under
the stairs, along the floor, a ragged gap let in
daylight. She glided to it. Dust flew as she beat
her wings to stop before it. The dust cloud
shimmered around her as she changed form
again.

She scurried across the floor. Her whiskers
twitched as she tested the size of the opening.
Tight but doable. She wriggled through to the

outside.

After the dark interior the sunlight was blinding. She blinked and waited for her eyes to adjust. Grass and wildflowers towered over her. Her nose twitched in vain, trying to catch scents that did not exist in dreams.

At the sound of raised voices coming from within the building, she startled and scampered into the grass. Moving as quickly as she could on her small legs, she headed away from the cabin.

Vibrations shook the ground and a shadow fell over her.

For one crucial moment she froze and something descended over her, entrapping her. She turned within the confined space. Fresh air and light came through a circle above her. She scrambled to the barrier and stood with her front paws braced against it. Cool and slightly damp, covered in a fine dusting of soil, the surface proved unyielding to her small nails.

"I've got her," a voice bellowed.

She shrank down on herself. Her body quivered in fear.

No, no, no.

She closed her eyes, held her breath, and concentrated. She felt her body ripple and then a disorienting sense of motion.

Human again, Lindsey tottered a few steps before coming to an unsteady halt. She could not open her eyes but felt certain she had changed locations. She heard gasps and people talking but could not make out the words.

In what felt like slow motion, she fell to her knees. As her body continued pitching forward, she sensed movement in front of her. Then she felt hands, *his* hands, on her shoulders, simultaneously slowing her fall and pulling her into an embrace, turning and moving with her until she was cradled in his lap.

Oh, thank God. She nearly sobbed with relief as she settled against his golden warmth.

"Shh," he soothed, touching his forehead to hers.

She struggled to open her eyes, to see him, but her eyelids felt like lead.

"Shh, don't fight it. Let yourself relax and go back to sleep," he urged.

I am asleep. I'm dreaming.

"No. Not really."

Lindsey tensed. This had to be a dream. What else could it be? But *he* was real. She felt certain of it. Had always believed it. He possessed a sense of presence not normally found in a dream. But so had the other man, the one who had tried to kill her twice now; he shared that quality with the man who held her. She fought the rising panic and struggled to ask the questions that were coming to mind.

"Please," he pleaded. "Let yourself sleep. I'll find you. I'll explain everything. I promise." He stroked her cheek. "Trust me."

She stilled at his words, wanting immediate answers but trusting him. Exhaustion overcame her and, secure against his chest, she let go of the dream and went back to sleep.

CHAPTER FOUR

LINDSEY SAT IN the booth with her laptop, sorting through Google search results, seeking answers to her dreams.

She had hardly slept in the past two weeks—she was scared to sleep. When she did finally give in to exhaustion, she was plagued by dream after dream. And although she had not woken with any more injuries, she was constantly hunted. Even awake she felt threatened. Occasionally, out of the corner of her eye, she would see a dark shape lurking, seeming to trail her. Whenever she tried to look directly at it, however, there would be nothing there.

Google had found over one million hits on lucid dreaming and nearly a million on feeling pain in dreams. She had tried various other searches with comparable results. She had skimmed through the more promising items, but nothing seemed to describe exactly what she was experiencing.

"Hey, Lindsey. Sorry I'm late." Dropping her tray on the table with a clatter of silverware, Makayla collapsed on the opposite bench. With a quick pinching motion, she picked a couple of pieces of lettuce and a cherry tomato off her tray and put them back in her salad. "Professor Mackey just would not stop. He kept going on and on about some tribe in South America, and it's not even going to be on the exam." Makayla stopped for a breath and looked at Lindsey. "You look awful. You feel all right?"

"Thanks," Lindsey deadpanned, shifting her computer and her own tray with french fries and a half-eaten burger to give Makayla more room. "I'm fine. Just tired."

"Late night?" Makayla inquired.

"I haven't been sleeping well. So what tribe in South America?" Lindsey asked, not wanting to discuss her recurring nightmares with Makayla.

Makayla rolled her eyes. "Who cares?" She grabbed her water bottle, removed the cap with a quick twist, and took a drink. Her cheeks puffed for a moment before she swallowed and continued, "Like I said, it's not on the exam. Just tell me what's on the freakin' exam and let me go already. Don't waste my time."

"Maybe he doesn't think it's a waste of time," Lindsey suggested as she scrolled through the Google search results.

"Whatever," Makayla muttered then asked with feigned nonchalance, "have you seen Jason lately?"

"Not for a few days and only in passing." Lindsey studied her friend and turned the question back to her. "Have you seen Jason lately?"

"No," Makayla said, not meeting Lindsey's eyes. "I've decided to make myself less available so maybe he'll appreciate me more."

"You're playing hard to get?" Lindsey asked incredulously.

"I wouldn't put it that way." Makayla pouted.

"Makayla, I don't think that's going to work," Lindsey said gently, thinking Jason would be overjoyed with her friend's new plan.

"Oh, Lindsey, does he like me at all?" Makayla asked desperately.

Lindsey resisted the impulse to tell Makayla that Jason must like her, or he would have had a restraining order issued against her by now. Instead, seeing the mix of hope and desperation in her friend's eyes, she weighed her words carefully.

"He's never said anything to make me think he sees you as anything other than a friend." At Makayla's crestfallen expression, Lindsey continued, "Why don't you try being his friend? Don't play games. Who knows, maybe something will change and he'll see you differently."

Clearly not happy with Lindsey's answer, Makayla nodded and poked at her salad with her fork.

"I'm sorry, Makayla. Would you rather I lied and told you I think your plan is brilliant, and that Jason will be your willing love slave before you know it?"

Makayla looked at Lindsey through her lashes and gave her a small smile. "Yes."

Fighting a smile of her own and struggling not to laugh, Lindsey said, "Your plan is brilliant. I'm sure he'll be your willing love slave in no time."

"Good! Then I'll finally be able to taste every yummy inch of him."

Lindsey pulled a face and put up a hand to keep her friend from going into detail.

Makayla gave her an exasperated look. "Come on, Lindsey. I know you've said it'd be like doing your brother, but you've got to admit he's hot."

"Thinking about Jason like that is..." Lindsey sought the right word. "Icky. It's right up there with thinking about my parents having sex. If by some chance you and Jason do hook up, you're going to have to find a new friend to share the details with."

Makayla looked at her with mingled disbelief and something that might have been disgust. "Why do I worry about you wanting him for yourself?"

"I don't know," Lindsey answered her friend, who sat shaking her head. Then Makayla's face suddenly lit up with a smile. Lindsey twisted in her seat and was not surprised to see Jason heading toward them.

Lindsey turned back to Makayla, who was already scooting over to make room for Jason. She considered reminding Makayla of her plan but quickly discarded the idea. She was already more in the middle than she wanted. She ran a finger over her computer's touchpad, stopping the geometric pattern of the screen saver and bringing back the results from her Google search.

"Ladies," Jason greeted them as he stepped next to their table. "May I join you?"

"Of course." Makayla beamed at him.

Lindsey gave him a quick smile before turning her attention back to her computer. "Just give me a minute to shut down and make room for you."

"You can sit next to me." Makayla patted her bench.

"Thanks, but I'll just sit here," he said, reaching around to a nearby table and pulling over a chair, missing Makayla's disappointed expression.

Lindsey closed her laptop and put it in the bag beside her. She pushed her tray aside. "There."

"Thanks." Jason put down his food.

"What were you working on?" Makayla asked.

"Entomology," Lindsey lied.

Jason lifted an eyebrow at her response, and Makayla gave her a puzzled look.

"Insects," Lindsey explained.

"Eww, your bug class." Makayla wrinkled her nose. "Remind me again why you're taking that class?"

"It fulfills a diversity requirement for my major. It's really pretty interesting," Lindsey replied before popping a french fry into her mouth.

"Uh-huh." Makayla turned to Jason. "How've you been?"

Lindsey missed his answer, her attention

drawn to a group of young men walking by their booth. She tried to fit one into the vague image she carried in her mind, but none matched the man in her dreams.

"...That's fabulous," Makayla squealed. "We'll be there. Won't we, Lindsey?"

Lindsey looked at them blankly. "I'm sorry?"

"Jason's band is playing at Dave's Dive," Makayla gushed.

"Great." Lindsey turned to Jason. "When?"

"Next Saturday. We take the stage at eight."

"I'll be there," Lindsey promised.

"Good." Jason nodded as he gave her a considering look.

Uncomfortable with his attention, Lindsey worked on finishing her lunch. Looking up only to scan the faces that moved past the table, she let Makayla's voice flow over her and barely registered Jason's responses.

"Well, guys, I need to go. Lindsey, get some sleep. Maybe get a sleep aid or something. You really do look awful." Makayla gathered her things and slid out of the booth. "See ya around."

Jason leaned back in his chair.

Lindsey squirmed under his gaze.

"What?" she blurted when the silence became too uncomfortable.

He lifted a shoulder. "I didn't know bugs dreamed."

Lindsey buried her face in her hands. "I didn't want to talk to Makayla about it. Okay?"

"You want to talk to me?"

"Not really."

"Linds."

"I said no." She slapped her palms on the table.

"Are you having nightmares again?"

"I don't want to talk about it."

"Makayla's right, you know. You look like shit."

"Gee, thanks." Her voice dripped sarcasm, and her eyes were daggers. "But I think she said I look awful."

"Yeah, but we know what she meant."

Lindsey groaned. "Jason, would you let it rest already?"

"Okay." He lifted his hands in surrender. "So, who've you been looking for?"

"I'm sorry?"

"You've been checking out every guy who's gone by. Who are you looking for? Have you met someone?"

Lindsey felt her cheeks grow warm. "No. No one."

Jason leaned forward and rested his elbows on the table. "Really." He looked at her intently.

"Yes, really." With quick, sharp motions Lindsey grabbed her things. "If you'll excuse me."

Moving quickly, Jason followed her.

"Come on, Lindsey. It's me. If you can't talk to me, who can you talk to?"

She shoved her trash in the can and slammed the tray down on top of it. With a false smile she faced Jason. "Has it ever occurred to you that sometimes it's because you're you that I don't talk to you?"

His lips moved as he silently tried to unravel her logic.

Lindsey turned on her heel and pushed her way out of the restaurant.

"Lindsey."

She stopped when he took ahold of her arm, but she stared straight ahead and refused to meet his eyes.

"Look, I'm sorry. You just seem really distracted, and you really do—"

Lindsey glared at him. "If you tell me again that I look like shit, I'm going to hit you."

His lips twitched and he shook his head. "I was going to say you really do look like you could use a good night's sleep."

"You'd be more convincing if you weren't trying so hard not to laugh," she said with narrowed eyes.

He hung his head, took a deep breath, and then looked at her. "I'm sorry, Linds. I've known you forever. I can tell something's bothering you. I worry." He reached up and brushed her cheek. "It worries me even more when you won't talk to me."

She sighed and looked away. "I haven't been sleeping well. That's all." When he said nothing, she glanced at him. Seeing the concern in his eyes, she felt a twinge of guilt at not telling him the truth, that she had been avoiding sleep and that what little sleep she got was far from restful. "I'm done with class for the day. I'll go home, get some sleep. Maybe I'll do like Makayla said and take something just to be sure I sleep. I'll be fine." She gave him a weak smile. "All right?"

Jason's jaw clenched, and he looked into the distance. His fingers tapped an agitated rhythm against his leg. He stilled abruptly and looked at her. "Yeah. Just do me a favor and don't take anything, okay? Just—just get some sleep."

Seeing the turmoil in his eyes, Lindsey knew he was thinking of her brother, Michael, remembering how he had overdosed. Jason pivoted, and she caught his arm before he could stalk away. She stepped close to him and waited for him to meet her gaze. "I'm not Mike. I'm talking about something you can pick up in a drugstore, not the hard stuff he did."

"I know. It's just—" He pinched the bridge of his nose then ran his hand over his head, disheveling his chocolate-colored hair. "I know Mike gave you grief about sleeping with the light on and having nightmares, but he had his own nightmares. I sometimes think that's why he started taking drugs."

Lindsey bit her lower lip, uncertain what to say.

Speaking so low Lindsey could hardly hear him, Jason continued in a gruff voice, "Losing Mike was like losing a brother. I couldn't handle losing you too." He put a hand behind her neck and kissed her on the forehead before resting his forehead on hers. "Be careful."

Lindsey nodded.

He gave her neck a gentle squeeze and left.

Lindsey watched his retreating back, thinking about what he had told her.

She had known Mike had nightmares. There had been many nights when she had lain awake afraid to go back to sleep and she would hear Mike cry out. Then she would hear him turn on his radio. She suspected that the only reason he never turned on a light was because, with their rooms across the hall from each other, her light filtered into his room—which had made his teasing all the more annoying. She had never considered the possibility that he had taken drugs because of the dreams.

Could Jason be right? Had Mike taken drugs to escape the nightmares? *I would've thought they'd make them worse.*

She let her feet carry her to the grocery store while her mind wrestled with the idea. Shadows skirted the edge of her vision as she walked.

At the store, Lindsey maneuvered through the aisles, around displays and other shoppers, filling her cart with a few essentials—a half gallon of milk, tea, chocolate Pop-Tarts. She was still uncertain she wanted to take anything, but she stopped in the pharmacy area and stood in front of row after row of small boxes, feeling overwhelmed by the choice.

Plucking one off the shelf at random, Lindsey read the tiny print on the back of the package. She returned it to the shelf and stood there staring.

I have no idea what to look for.

"You could take an antihistamine."

Lindsey turned to find a middle-aged woman in a pharmacy coat standing behind her. "Excuse me?"

"The active ingredient in half the sleep aids is the same, and it tends to cost less," the woman explained. "You'll need to take two to get the same dosage."

"Thanks," Lindsey replied.

The woman nodded, grabbed something off the shelf, and went to speak with a frazzled-looking young woman balancing an infant on her hip.

Lindsey scanned the shelves for the allergy medications. Not finding them, she tried the next aisle and found them on the bottom shelf. She bent over to grab a box and saw a movement out of the corner of her eye. Figuring it was another shopper or a piece of her hair, Lindsey ignored it, but then she heard a single word uttered, a whisper soft and full of menace.

"Kitten."

A cold, prickling sensation ran over her scalp and down her back as Lindsey slowly straightened. With great trepidation, she turned.

One of the men who had chased her through the woods, a figure from her nightmare, stood before her hefting a two-headed axe.

Lindsey squeezed her eyes shut tight.

He won't be there. It's in my head. He won't be

there.

She opened her eyes.

He was still there with the axe raised high.

Lindsey backed up a step, running into the shelves and toppling a couple of boxes. She was unable to look away as the axe came down. Just before striking her, the axe and its wielder vanished. Dazed, she stared at the spot where the man had stood.

This has to end. She tossed the medicine into her cart. With shaking hands she replaced the boxes she had knocked over.

She paid for her groceries and hurried home.

After putting everything where it belonged, Lindsey got a glass of water and opened the . She removed two capsules. Inexplicably nervous, she held them in her palm for a moment, but the hope, the need, for a sound night of sleep compelled her to swallow them one after the other.

She put on her pajamas and crawled into bed.

CHAPTER FIVE

LINDSEY WAS IN the biology lab. Three rows of black countertops with inset sinks, stools lining their lengths, ran down the center of the room. Baking pans filled with black wax rested before each stool. The lab was well lit, and everything seemed in place.

She sat at the end of one of the counters, an empty dissection tray before her. She heard a repetitive soft thumping behind her. Looking over her shoulder, Lindsey saw a dragonfly repeatedly bumping into the window.

Outside, the sun shone, birds flew between the trees, and the occasional leaf tumbled in the wind.

Putting her hand on the counter, Lindsey got to her feet intending to go outside and enjoy the beautiful day. She took a few steps toward the window then hesitated. How was she going to get outside? There were no doors, she noted with annoyance. With a sigh she considered the window. *Why not?*

Lindsey intended to grab a stool and break the window, but when she reached for one, her hand closed on empty air. Surprised, she turned to find another stool or something else to shatter the glass. The lab was now gone, replaced with someone's living room.

Vaguely familiar, the room was dark, lit only with the silver-grey of moonlight. Heavy wooden beams crossed the ceiling, traversing the length of the living room into the dining room straight ahead. A coffee table sat directly in front of her. To her left was a faux fireplace flanked by some kind of chair.

Lindsey looked at it more closely, expecting to see a recliner, but instead there was a rocking chair with a faded blue and white quilt draped over the back. At the sight of the quilt, she felt a frisson of fear and her stomach knotted. She took a hasty step back and caught her leg on the edge of an old sofa. She tumbled onto its thick cushions. As she struggled to escape its depths, the room lightened.

Lindsey froze as her shadow grew, stretching across the coffee table before her.

She remembered.

She remembered this place, this dream.

She knew the source of the light.

It terrified her every time.

Moving with exaggerated slowness, afraid of drawing attention to herself, she rose from the sofa. She looked over her shoulder at the window framed by heavy drapes with the sheers closed. Two circles of light shone through them.

There was a rumbling sound she felt rather than heard.

Never taking her eyes from the window, Lindsey moved around the coffee table and backed into the dining room.

The twin circles grew larger.

The walls began to reverberate.

Her heart pounding, she slid around the table and chairs until she stood next to an archway leading to the kitchen.

For a moment everything stopped: the rumbling ceased and the light held steady.

The moment stretched. Then snapped.

The cab of a semi burst through the window, bouncing over the couch like a monster truck over a series of cars. Glass flew, and Lindsey felt it hitting her as she dove into the kitchen.

She landed hard on the floor, but knowing

that the semi would pursue her relentlessly, its mass impossibly fitting in the halls and through the doorways, she scrambled to her feet and ran through the house. She closed doors behind her in hopes of slowing the vehicle down, but the machine followed her with ease, shattering doors and doorframes, sending cascades of debris before it that showered upon her head and back.

In a bedroom Lindsey found a sliding glass door to the backyard. She fumbled with the latch and shoved the pane to one side. Once outside, she immediately turned to the right.

The truck barreled after her, and more glass flew.

Her bare arms covered in stinging cuts, Lindsey ran to the front of the house, cutting through flower beds. Lights from behind threw her shadow in front of her, long and thin. Arms and legs pumping in tandem, her chest aching, she raced down the street. Inexplicably, she maintained her lead. She turned down the first side street she reached.

Once out of sight of the truck, Lindsey bolted into the bushes and made her way to the side of a house. Carefully, she opened the gate to the backyard and slipped inside. Hugging the wall and keeping to the shadows, she made her way to the back of the house.

Crouched behind a bush, she struggled to catch her breath and tried to figure out how to get away. She could neither see nor hear the semi, but she knew it was still there.

Gathering her courage, she bolted across the back lawn, an open expanse except for a swing set and the bushes against the house. She reached the chain link fence in the back and with some effort scrambled over it. Her feet hit the ground, and she was bathed in light.

The truck appeared out of nowhere. With a roar of the engine, it came at her full throttle.

Backed against the fence, she turned her head away from the oncoming vehicle. She squeezed her eyes shut and held her breath, waiting for the impact that would wake her.

A rippling sense of motion filled her, the push-pull of the ocean tide building inside her, a crescendo that at its peak had her feeling squeezed and stretched.

The staccato of gunfire replaced the engine's roar. The chain link fence became cold brick. A bullet ricocheted off the wall near her head, sending a fragment flying, scoring her cheek.

The pain roused her to action. She took shelter behind a derelict car. Pressed close to its paint-chipped, rust-pitted side, Lindsey surveyed the area.

Skyscrapers loomed over her. Tattered remnants of blinds hung outside missing windows. Few streetlights shone. Cars lined the street. Gunfire sounded at regular intervals. She could see the occasional figure moving furtively from shadow to shadow.

Keeping a wary eye on where the gunshots seemed to originate, she inched her way along the car, moving in the opposite direction. At the fender she paused and looked behind her. *Where do I go?*

Lindsey considered the various storefronts. Many of them had doors hanging ajar. None of them felt familiar or evoked a sense of safety.

She looked down the line of cars. There was an intersection half a block away. Maybe there would be something more promising on the other street.

Keep moving.

Bent over and fighting the urge to make a run for it, she slowly crossed the distance. When she neared the intersection, she left the relative safety of the cars and sprinted to the nearest building. Crouching, she peered around the corner. While the area looked every bit as war torn, she saw no signs of movement and heard no gunfire.

Lindsey slowly straightened as she rounded the building, half expecting to get shot or
to have the semi reappear. When nothing happened, she moved down the sidewalk searching
for a likely place to take shelter.

She walked for blocks, passing several places that she could see no reason for not entering, but something inside her rebelled when she
approached them. Weary and aching, she kept
going until a sudden movement caught her eye.
She froze and tried to find what she had seen.
There.

Across the street, next to the newsstand:
was there something there? Looking directly at
the spot, she saw nothing, but when she angled
her head ever so slightly and let her eyes unfo-
cus, the shadows deepened and pulsed. Judging
it wise to give the area a wide berth, she eased
back a step.

Someone grabbed her upper arm and pulled
her back.

Off balance and unable to lunge forward as
instinct demanded, she crashed against a hard
body.

A hand clamped over her mouth, muffling
her scream before it could escape and echo off
the walls. She clawed at it to no avail. With an

arm now wrapped around her waist she was dragged backward several feet and pulled into one of the buildings.

"It's okay."

Lindsey stilled, recognizing *his* voice.

"It's me, Nathan." He removed his hand from her mouth, but instead of releasing her, he put his arm around her, embracing her from behind.

She relaxed into his golden warmth and tipped her head back against his shoulder. When the fear and panic subsided, she raised her hand and curled her fingers around his wrist. With a subtle squeeze she silently asked him to let her go.

He freed her with seeming reluctance: his arms loosened slowly and fell from her, and then he placed his hands on her shoulders, ran them down to her elbows, and squeezed gently before putting distance between them.

She glanced over her shoulder and watched him walk to the entrance and peer around the door. He stood still as if watching something.

Probably the dark spot.

With a sigh Lindsey scanned the area. She stood next to a counter with a cash register. A couple of riding lawn mowers sat in an open area under the broken front window. Shelves lined the walls and stood in three even rows down the center of the store. Most of the shelves were empty, but from what remained Lindsey guessed they were in a hardware store.

Looking at the riding mowers again, she wondered why a store in the middle of a city would stock them. It made no sense, but then dreams rarely did.

Not seeing a better place to sit, she sank to the floor and leaned against the counter. She glanced at Nathan, who was still keeping his watch. Confident he would tell her when they needed to move, she put her head back and closed her eyes.

Nathan. She tried his name in her mind, feeling a rush of pleasure in finally knowing it.

"What the hell happened to you?" He tentatively touched her scraped cheek.

She opened her eyes at the contact, surprised to see him crouched before her.

"There was a truck, and—" Lindsey stopped short as she realized she could see Nathan: his features were not the typical blur. She marveled at being able to gaze at him, but at his expectant look she finished, "Then I think someone shot at me."

"I can't believe you haven't woken up," he muttered as he pulled her to her feet and started leading her to the back door. "You need to get out of here. Wake yourself up."

"I don't think I can. I took a sleeping pill."

He whirled to face her. The color drained from his face, and fear filled his blue eyes. He grabbed her by the shoulders and shook her. "Are you insane?"

He released her, covered his eyes with his hands, and rubbed them down over his face. He walked in a tight circle muttering obscenities.

"I'm starting to think so," she answered in a small voice. He seemed not to hear.

He came back and stood in front of her.

His expression was unreadable, but she could feel waves of turmoil coming from him. He raked his hand through his hair, then grabbed her hand and tugged her after him.

Going out the back door of the hardware store, Nathan led her into an alley and continued out into the city once more. He moved quickly and she struggled to keep pace with him.

After several blocks, out of breath and feeling the beginnings of a cramp in her side, she planted her feet and yanked him to a stop.

"Nathan, please. I can't keep going like this." She dropped his hand and bent over, putting her hands on her knees.

"Fine." He sounded as out of breath as she

felt. "Let's at least get off the street."

She nodded, and the pair made their way to the mouth of an alley. They stopped when they reached the shadows inside it.

Breathing normally again, she asked, "Where are we going?"

Before Nathan could answer, they heard a sound that caused them to turn and look at the entrance of the alley.

Goose bumps formed on Lindsey's arms.

She could feel something dark moving toward them.

Nathan took her arm above the elbow and drew her behind him. He slid his hand down to take hers in a firm grip. At his silent urging she stepped cautiously back further into the alley, carefully placing her feet to avoid debris.

A shape loomed at the alley's entrance.

Lindsey's back hit a wall. She turned her head to search for a way out and felt sick to her stomach when she realized they were trapped.

She turned to tell Nathan as he stepped back into her. She put her free hand on his shoulder, and he continued moving until the full length of their bodies were pressed together. Lindsey could not see over his shoulder, but she heard a shuffling sound and heavy breathing. Her own breath came fast and shallow as Nathan's weight crushed her into the wall.

He reached around her with his free hand and placed it on the wall, fingers splayed.

She gasped as the bricks softened behind her.

Nathan leaned his weight into her, and she felt the brick give. It was like sinking into a down comforter and just as suffocating, as he maneuvered her further into the wall until she was surrounded by unbroken darkness. Only his fierce grip on her hand gave her any sense of solidity.

Right before panic overtook her, the black gave way to grey, and she nearly fell as she emerged on the other side. She watched as he finished stepping through the wall. It seemed unchanged by their passing. He paused for a moment before turning to her.

"How?" she asked.

"We all have our tricks," he answered with a slight smile, giving her hand a quick caress with his thumb. "Come on."

CHAPTER SIX

HAND IN HAND they moved through the streets, Nathan leading with easy familiarity. Twice they backtracked when they encountered more of the pulsing black spots. Several times they took cover when they heard gunfire. After what felt like hours, they came to the outskirts of the city, and Nathan drew them to a stop.

"We're here." He gestured ahead of them.

Across the street, nestled beneath an overpass and surrounded by pavement with knee-high grass growing in the cracks, sat a train-car diner. It was painted silver and red, and while not brightly lit, it was somehow clearer and stood in sharp contrast to its surroundings.

"This is one of my places," Nathan said.

"The city?" Lindsey asked in surprise.

"No, just the diner." Under his breath so she barely heard him, he added, "I hope it's enough."

Nathan scanned the area, presumably checking for trouble before crossing the street, and Lindsey, following his example, cast a quick glance behind her.

"Let's go," he said as he put a hand on the small of her back. Together they crossed the open space. When they reached the diner, he let her enter first then closed and locked the door behind him.

Lindsey glanced around the small restaurant. A jukebox sat to her immediate left by the door. Its playlist was dark and no music emanated from it. A half dozen round, backless stools sat in front of a red counter that ran half the length of the diner before giving way to a couple of booths. Under the front windows were several small, round red-topped tables with two chrome-backed chairs at each one.

Lindsey followed Nathan to a booth near the restrooms and the rear exit. They sat opposite each other.

"We should be safe here for a while," he said, peering somewhat anxiously out the windows.

Lindsey studied him, drinking in her fill and trying to memorize his features against the probability of them once more being blurred the next time they met. What struck her the most were his eyes. Surrounded by thick dark lashes, they were a deep, azure blue that reminded Lindsey of Caribbean seas.

His hair was dark, but the dim lighting made it hard to determine if it was black or brown. It curled slightly against his forehead and over his ears. It looked like it would just brush his collar if he were wearing a dress shirt instead of the black T-shirt he now wore.

Nathan grabbed a napkin from the dispenser, leaned forward with his elbows resting on the table, and proceeded to shred the napkin. Fixing her with those startling blue eyes, he spoke in a low, urgent tone. "Listen. You have to wake up as soon as you can. Until then, keep moving. Things have changed since..." He looked away from her and absently brushed the shredded bits aside. He met her gaze again, his expression grim. "You can die here."

Lindsey's brow furrowed. She felt like she was missing something. "I've died in dreams before," she began. "It's not fun, and I'd rather not do it, but it's not like—" She waved her hand. "It's not like it's true that if you die in a dream, you die for real. You just wake up."

Nathan shook his head adamantly. "I know what you mean, but Lindsey, I'm telling you things have changed."

"Changed how?" Lindsey's stomach knotted with dread.

"We can't be here for prolonged periods without risking injuries that cross into the physical world, and there are things, people, who can kill you."

Lindsey thoughtfully touched her still-bruised abdomen.

"Lindsey, you have to wake up, and if you can't do that, then you need to run until you can. Avoid confrontations. You've always had a good bag of tricks for getting out of tight spots." Nathan looked out the windows and murmured, "You're probably going to need them all."

"No," she snapped, drawing his attention to her. "I mean, I know I do things but I don't know how I do them. I have no control. They just happen."

"I wish..." he began, but then turned once more to the window. His whole body tensed and he slid out of the booth. He shot her a look filled with concern. "There's no more time. I'm sorry I can't explain now. Trust yourself. Trust your instincts."

She slid out to stand in front of him. Feeling like a coward for even asking, she pleaded with him. "Stay with me."

He cupped her cheek then ran his fingers through her hair. His eyes filled with sorrow as he tracked the motion. "I would if I could, but sooner or later I will wake up whether I mean to or not."

She started to protest, but Nathan shook his head.

"You need to go," he insisted. "I'll stay and distract them as long as I can."

He looked to the windows again, and Lindsey turned to look as well. A wall of darkness blocked out everything on the other side of the street, as if the city had disappeared behind a black curtain. The darkest areas pulsed ominously and filled Lindsey with foreboding.

She turned back to Nathan and found him watching her with a hungry gaze. Her body thrummed in response, danger forgotten for the moment.

He gave himself a shake and her a weak smile.

As he headed to the door, he told her, "There are others like us. Other dreamstriders. They'll help as they can. You'll recognize them. Just like you do with me."

Lindsey slowly trailed after him with a sinking feeling.

With his hand on the door, Nathan paused and took a deep breath, to all appearances bracing himself for what was to come. A sword appeared in his hand, and Lindsey recognized it. She knew she had seen him wield it before.

Their eyes met.

"Stay safe," he whispered.

She nodded shakily. "You, too."

With determination etched in his features, Nathan exited the diner. Panic flooded Lindsey as she watched him leave. She rushed to the door to call him back.

"Nathan," she cried. She flung open the door only to find nothing lay beyond the opening. She stared in disbelief, and her mind spun frantically. The darkness had all the depth of the night sky but no reassuring pinpricks of starlight.

Now what? Lindsey asked herself.

Run, Nathan's voice sounded in her mind.

She stood uncertainly. Had she really heard him?

Lindsey, run! This time, she had no doubt it was really him.

Chills ran up her spine with the feeling that she was no longer alone in the diner.

She heard a footfall behind her.

A cold wind blew from the rear exit.

Lindsey wrapped her arms around herself.

What had Nathan told her?

We all have our tricks...You've always had a good bag of tricks for getting out of tight spots...Trust your instincts.

"Lindsey," purred a voice behind her, a voice she recognized and dreaded.

She whirled to face the man she knew to be an enemy. The corner of his mouth quirked in a mocking half smile as he toyed with a dagger, tossing it in low, lazy arcs, alternately catching it by the blade and the grip.

Focusing her attention inward, she willed herself to be anywhere but the diner. She had the satisfaction of seeing her nemesis's smile fade and his face darken with anger as the rippling sensation gripped her and carried her elsewhere.

When the rippling ceased, Lindsey ignored her surroundings. Instead, she willed herself away again, desperate to put distance between herself and her foe. She continued to push herself from one location to the next.

A couple of times, she arrived in a place where she sensed another presence. In these places, she lingered, remembering Nathan's assurance that others would help her, but when she tried to approach them they drifted away, causing her to question if they had been there at all.

Frustrated and fatigued, Lindsey pushed onward until she burst into sunlight high above a valley. Shock caused her to falter, but then she realized where she was—what she was. With a joyful cry, she spread her wings, and the air currents carried her aloft. She let the exhilaration of flight storm through her as she soared over the verdant green valley with the clouds as her only companions. She delighted in the cool breeze that ruffled the short feathers on her chest and gently tugged the stiff pinions on her wings. She looked down into the valley. Her sharp eyes picked out minute details among the tall grass that swayed and undulated like the sea: a nesting quail, a skittish rabbit. With the twitch of a tail feather, she caught another current and changed direction, luxuriating in the peace and serenity of flight. It was the closest thing to heaven she had ever known.

Without warning, pain ripped through her, radiating from her left wing near her chest. Her shriek nearly muffled the sound of the gun's report. She plunged from the sky, helplessly buffeted by the winds.

Her vision became a white blur as she shifted between hawk and human and back again.

She was too tired to force herself into one shape or the other and was uncertain it would make a difference what form she took: if she hit the ground, if she failed to wake up before impact, she was certain she would die as Nathan had said.

Lindsey closed her eyes. Thoughts of her parents, Jason, Makayla, and Nathan flooded her mind.

God, please, she prayed, *I'm not ready. Let me wake up. Wake up, wake up, WAKE UP!*

She felt the long grass brush against her.

CHAPTER SEVEN

SWORD IN HAND, Nathan left the diner and faced the creatures stepping out of the darkness: giant beasts that stood at least seven feet tall. He counted eight of them as they fanned out around him.

Wanting more room to maneuver, he moved forward, putting some distance between himself and the diner.

Some of the creatures sidled around to flank him. They moved with a surprisingly supple grace despite their massive builds.

Nathan was determined to buy time for Lindsey, but he had no illusions about his chances against the hulking forms.

Although they were roughly human-shaped, their arms appeared abnormally long and were covered with greenish-brown tufts that reminded Nathan of moss. Their eyes had the gold-red reflective glow of animals, and a few of them had short, yellowed tusks protruding from their mouths. Each carried a weapon that matched their size: bardiches with long curved blades on one end of a staff and an axe head on the other, halberds, long hand-and-a-half swords.

This is going to be ugly, Nathan thought grimly as he raised his blade. He waited for them to come at him.

They stood, poised ready to strike, but made no move to attack.

Puzzled by their inaction, Nathan flexed his fingers around the hilt.

What are they waiting for? He shifted his weight from foot to foot then held still. He tilted his head, thinking he had heard his name.

A gust of arctic cold hit him from behind.

He spun without thinking.

The diner had been swallowed by the darkness. A malicious glee emanated from where it had stood.

Thinking of Lindsey, he stepped toward the absent diner.

Run. He willed her to hear him. *Lindsey, run!*

He continued to head where the diner had been, determined to get back to it. It was his place. He had an affinity for it. No one could keep him from going there.

In his concern for Lindsey, he forgot the creatures behind him until he heard the sound of their approach. He pivoted, barely raising his sword in time to stop a crushing blow. He forced his assailant back and swung his sword wide, striking one of the creatures and drawing a stinking black ooze. He willed a dagger into his free hand then planted it up to the quillon into his opponent's hide.

There were too many, however, and they soon pulled him down.

When one of the blades pierced his flesh, he flinched from the pain and woke up, as he had known he inevitably would.

Nathan stared blankly at the ceiling as his breathing steadied. Throwing back the covers, he got up and made his way to the bathroom. He splashed some water on his face and raked damp hands through his hair. Running his hand over his bare ribs where pain still lingered, he found a small red welt that would undoubtedly reveal a bruise later.

He had gotten out of the dream in time to avoid serious injury. Would Lindsey be as lucky? Would whatever she had taken to help her sleep have worn off enough to let her escape? He somberly met his gaze in the mirror.

"You've really fucked up," he told his reflection. He should never have left her alone in the diner. He should have stayed by her side as long as he could.

His toes curling away from the cold wood floor, Nathan went to the kitchen and got a glass of water before returning to bed.

He punched his pillow and stretched out, hoping to fall back to sleep so he could search for Lindsey.

Filled with anxiety, he tossed and turned.

You should've left her alone, he scolded himself. He should never have drawn her back into the dream realm. For all her skill, she had never been comfortable there, had never been happy being a dreamstrider. And with good reason. How many times had he come upon her as she fled some horror?

He had happily played guardian angel until another dreamstrider suggested that Nathan was the only reason Lindsey continued to return to the dream realm night after night despite her obvious fear. The idea simultaneously appealed to him and appalled him. Being with Lindsey, as corny as it sounded to him, was like being with his soul mate. Nathan never felt more alive. When he was with her, the worries of the waking world fell away and the possibilities in the dream realm seemed endless. But he was unwilling to ask her to go through nightly terror.

He had withdrawn from her—had let her believe he was dead—and she had stopped dreamstriding.

Despite his resolve to leave her be, Nathan never stopped watching for her, asleep or awake.

When things began to change, his first thought was to warn her. The others had told him not to go to her, although he knew their reasons for keeping their distance were far different from his own. He had told her the others would help because he wanted to believe they would. He knew, however, that they might not. They feared Lindsey.

Enough of this. Go back to sleep already.

He covered his eyes with his arm.

His thoughts shied away from the possibility that Lindsey could already be dead. Agitated, he flung his arm from his eyes and flipped onto his stomach. The red display of his digital clock illuminated the surface of the nightstand. Nathan reached over and hit the sleep button to turn on the radio. The soft strains of a piano concerto reached his ears. Soothed by the music and worn out with worry, he fell asleep thinking of Lindsey.

He entered the dream on the edge of a clearing, an old-growth forest at his back. He scanned the area, desperate for any sign of Lindsey. He could *feel* her nearby.

Hearing a hawk's cry, he searched the sky. With horror he saw a hawk plummeting. The wind buffeted her, tumbling her this way and that as she fell.

Lindsey.

Fear coursed through him, hit him so hard he nearly lost the dream. He dashed across the glade, crashed through the underbrush, and wove between the trees, racing to where Lindsey was falling. He lost sight of her as the canopy thickened. Hoping he still moved in the right direction, Nathan hastened forward. When he broke through the trees, his eyes raked the sky.

There she was—just above tree height— flickering between hawk and human. Leading with head and shoulders, she looked like she was going to slam into the ground on her neck and upper back. There seemed little chance she would hold the hawk form long enough to tent her wings and land safely, and Nathan was too far away to catch her.

"No," he protested in a strangled voice as she neared the ground. Paralyzed by fear, he watched her crash.

When she struck the ground, the dream rippled from the point of impact like a pond disturbed by a stone and nearly knocked Nathan off his feet. He plowed through the tall grass feeling like he was moving through water. He reached the spot where Lindsey had hit.

Bloody feathers lay amid the flattened and broken stems, but she was not there.

Nathan dropped to his knees in relief.

Shakily, he picked up one of the feathers. Droplets of blood clung to it, obscuring the lines between the alternating bands of rust-brown and white. He put it in his palm and curled his fingers around it. He could feel an echo of Lindsey through the feather.

He had to find her in the real world. He had to make sure she understood what was happening. He had to make sure she was okay. He had to make sure she was whole.

But how? Could it be done?

Nathan had considered the problem before. It seemed like an impossible task. The world was a big place, and the dream realm did not always mirror the physical world. It was too easily influenced by the dreamers themselves: shaped by their experiences and imaginings, their hopes and fears.

He looked down at his hand.

She had never left a piece of herself behind before.

Nathan thought of Lindsey, recalled the feel of her, the feel of sun-warmed skin kissed by a cool breeze. He felt a resonance with the feather, a pulsing warmth against his palm. He opened his hand and watched the feather dissolve into his flesh until nothing remained but a faint, shimmering mark.

He and Lindsey had shared a connection before, but he suspected they were now irrevocably bound to each other. Or, at least, he to her.

Feelings flooded him: fear and confusion followed by the incredible joy and freedom of flight, so that for the first time he understood her preference for the hawk form. Not nearly as cumbersome as flying as a human, it was the difference between effortless ecstasy and awkward endeavor.

Then, searing pain cauterized his senses.

Darkness descended upon him for a heartbeat. Images flashed through his mind too fast to decipher, but he took them all into himself. He held on to them tightly, knowing they were the key to finding Lindsey.

He woke.

Sunlight spilled through gaps in the shades,

and he could hear the rumbling of the recycling truck moving down the street.

Nathan considered the images he had seen. They were a tangled mess in his mind, but he would sort them out. He would find Lindsey.

He prayed she was okay.

CHAPTER EIGHT

HI, THIS IS Lindsey. I can't get to the phone. Leave a message...

Beep. "Hi, Lindsey. I was just calling to see how your week has been. Your dad and I are going to dinner with the Moores tonight, so I'll talk to you tomorrow."

Beep. "Lindsey Allison Trent, I cannot believe you stood me up. Remember, Monday? Lunch with Makayla? Look, if there's a hot guy involved, all's forgiven, but if I had lunch by myself because of your bug class or something, you're buying for the rest of the month. Call me."

Beep. "Uh, yeah, um, Lindsey, this is Josh. I thought we had a tutoring thing this afternoon, but you weren't there so maybe I got it wrong. Anyway, I got this exam this Friday and I need some help. So could you call me?"

Beep. "Hi, honey, it's Mom. Sorry I missed you. Give me a call when you get a chance."

Beep. "Lindsey? Honey? I kind of thought I'd hear from you by now. Call me."

Beep. "Lindsey. Jason. My mom got a call from your mom wanting to know if I had said anything about how you were lately. Apparently, your mother is worried about you because you haven't called her in a while. So now my mom is worried...you know how it goes. I promised to drop by after I was done here, so if you don't want company, give me a call on my cell."

Beep. "Uh, Lindsey, this is Josh again. My test is like *two* days away. Call me. *Please.*"

CHAPTER NINE

THE POUNDING WOULD not stop.

Lindsey grudgingly opened her eyes then gingerly rubbed the sleep out of them with a shaky right hand.

Weak light seeped into the room around the blinds, suggesting it was early morning or evening, but then, given it was fall verging on winter, it could have been noon and overcast.

She glanced at the clock—4:30 p.m. Evening, then.

The pounding continued, and she thought she heard a muffled shout that might have been her name.

Someone's at the door, she realized.

She cautiously sat up in her bed, waiting for the dizziness and nausea to return. When she managed to straighten without either, she breathed a sigh of relief.

With shuffling steps she made her way through the dimly lit apartment.

She winced with each knock on the door.

With fumbling fingers, she opened it a crack and squinted outside to see Jason. Without a word, she released the doorknob and walked back the way she had come, leaving the door ajar.

"Lindsey?" Jason's voice followed her down the hall.

Not bothering with the lights, she let her momentum carry her to the bathroom.

After using the toilet, Lindsey stood in front of the sink. Studiously avoiding her image in the mirror, she ran her tongue over her teeth—they definitely needed brushing. She took care of her teeth and combed the fingers of her right hand through her hair, cringing at the greasy feel of it.

It's gonna have to do, she told herself as she left the bathroom.

She stepped into her slippers and put on her robe before going out to face Jason.

Experimentally, she moved her left arm as she walked. Motion at the shoulder was excruciating, but the rest of her arm, if still a little tingly, seemed to be doing better.

Jason had turned on a lamp.

"Have you been sick?" he asked as she emerged into the light. Then his eyes widened and his jaw clenched. He paled slightly before flushing with emotion.

His reaction confirmed Lindsey's suspicion that she still looked pretty rough, to say the least. She was glad she had put on her robe and concealed the purple-black mark on her shoulder.

"My God, Linds. How—? What—?" Jason put a hand to his mouth and took a deep breath around it. He exhaled raggedly, dropping his fisted hand.

"Who did this to you?" he asked in a tight voice.

Lindsey stepped around him and sank onto the sofa, tipping her head back and letting her eyes drift closed. What could she tell him? How could she possibly explain? The truth sounded ludicrous.

"Lindsey," he barked, losing control.

"Nathan, please don't yell," Lindsey implored, raising a hand to rub her forehead, feeling an impending headache.

"Nathan? Who's Nathan?" he demanded.

"Jason. I said Jason," she hastily amended.

"No, you said Nathan. Who is he? Did *he* do this to you?" His voice dropped almost to a growl.

"No." Her eyes flew open as she forcibly denied Nathan's responsibility.

Their gazes locked.

Lindsey could practically hear Jason grinding his teeth, and he had a wild look in his eyes.

I'm going to have to tell him the truth. The realization did not sit well with her, but she had no plausible story prepared. She doubted he would be happy with the truth, whether he believed her or not.

"Jason, please sit."

He sat in front of her on the coffee table, his legs on either side of hers. He leaned forward, elbows on thighs, waiting for her to speak.

She drew in a calming breath.

"Friday," she began then stopped. Her brow furrowed. "What's today?"

"Wednesday," Jason choked out.

Lindsey nodded.

"Friday," she started again. "After I left you, I went to the store and got an allergy med to help me sleep." Seeing his puzzled look, she rushed to explain. "The pharmacist told me it was the same as the sleeping pills. Who knew?

"Anyway, I wasn't sure I was going to take anything, but while I was in the store, I saw this man with this giant axe, and he was standing there swinging the thing at me one minute, the next he was gone. I've seen this guy before in nightmares. I figured if I was starting to see things, hallucinate, I really needed to get some sleep."

Jason's eyes narrowed as he listened.

Lindsey paused, and Jason put a hand on her knee and gently squeezed it, silently urging her to continue. Fearing the disbelief she felt certain would be in his eyes, Lindsey looked down at her lap. She swallowed hard and spoke in a rush.

"When I got home, I went to bed and had this really, really nasty nightmare. There was this truck chasing me, and then I was in some city and there were bullets flying." She gestured absently at her cheek. "And then...then I was shot out of the sky and fell and crashed, I think. I woke up and..." Lindsey bit her lip, remembering the consuming pain and panic.

She had woken sucking in great gulping breaths, feeling like she could not get enough air. Her entire body had ached. Her left shoulder had been the worst, throbbing with every heartbeat, yet the rest of her left arm had been frighteningly void—a dead weight at her side. When she had tried to get up to go to the bathroom, the room had spun violently. Somehow she had reached her goal, just in time for her stomach to heave, wracking her already-tender frame.

"Lindsey," Jason softly recalled her to the present.

Hesitantly, she met his gaze.

"Are you telling me you got hurt in a dream?" His tone was carefully neutral.

"Yes," she whispered.

"Linds, people don't get hurt by dreams. Is it possible—" He raised a hand to stop her protest. "Is it possible someone broke in while you were sleeping and attacked you? That you're suppressing what happened and confusing it with a dream?"

Lindsey emphatically shook her head.

Jason sagged a bit, concern in his eyes. He looked down then asked, "Who's Nathan? You've never mentioned him before."

She bit her lip and turned to watch her goldfish swim in lazy circles.

The silence grew uncomfortable.

Lindsey fidgeted in her seat.

She glanced at Jason then flicked her eyes away, unwilling to meet his scrutinizing gaze.

"You told me he didn't do this to you," Jason prompted.

"He didn't. He would never..." Lindsey

looked directly into Jason's eyes, begging him to believe her. "He's always protected me."

Jason slowly straightened, withdrawing his hand from Lindsey's knee.

"You've known him for a while then?" His tone was troubled.

"Yes. From dreams," she reluctantly admitted. "He's always been there."

Jason stood and began to pace the small area.

Lindsey drew her knees up to her chest, curling in on herself.

"Have you seen a doctor?" he asked.

"No," she answered in a small voice.

"Of course not," he snarled.

Lindsey cringed at the frustration in his voice.

"I couldn't," she explained. "How could I tell them what I told you? You don't believe me, and you've known me my entire life." Bitterness tinged her words. "I'd end up with a psych consult and observation."

"Might be a good idea," Jason muttered.

Lindsey scowled at him and finished, "And, if I fed them some story, they'd probably need to make a report to the police."

Jason stopped pacing and faced Lindsey.

"This is crazy," he told her.

"I know how it sounds."

"Do you expect me to believe you?"

"No, not really, but I hoped you would."

Jason threw his hands out and started pacing again, muttering to himself.

Lindsey looked into the kitchen and read the time off the microwave clock—it had been long enough that she could have more ibuprofen. She scooted off the couch. Jason started toward her as if to offer her help, but she waved him away. His regard weighed heavily upon her as she went into the kitchen and got a glass of water.

She had left the ibuprofen next to the stove. The lid sat loose upon the bottle.

It had been five of the most frustrating minutes of her life trying to figure out how to open the childproof lid with only one hand—wedging the bottle between her hip and the corner of the counter—and she preferred not having to do it every time she needed more painkillers.

Lindsey removed the lid and tipped the bottle.

Nothing came out.

She looked in the bottle in disbelief then started opening all the cabinets, hoping to find a forgotten bottle.

"Lindsey."

She jumped at the sound of Jason's voice.

"What do you need?" he gently inquired.

"I'm out of ibuprofen."

"I could go get some for you," he offered.

"I'd appreciate it." Her voice was strained. Why did her headache seem so much worse now that she would have to wait to take something?

Jason put his hand on her left shoulder.

She caught her breath, looked away, and struggled not to flinch from his touch: seeing the bruise on her shoulder would only set him off again, and she was tired.

"I'm sorry," he said, apparently taking her actions as a rebuff, and letting his hand fall to his side. "Is there anything else I can get for you?"

"Could you pick up some food for tonight and the morning? I'll make myself go to the store tomorrow."

"I can do that for you. Can I stay for dinner?"

Lindsey gave him a small smile. "Only if you cook."

"Deal," he agreed with a smile of his own.

"Let me get my purse." She moved around him and headed for her room.

"I can take care of it," he protested.

"You don't have to. Besides, I'm guessing you don't have your key, since you were trying to break the door down instead of just letting yourself in," she countered over her shoulder.

"True," he admitted.

Lindsey grabbed her keys and pulled a twenty and a handful of ones out of her wallet. She took them to Jason and found him rummaging through her fridge, putting aside containers that obviously had things growing in them.

"Here." She put the keys and cash on the counter.

He gave her a brief glance before turning back to the refrigerator. "Thanks."

"I'm going to take a shower."

"Okay." He sniffed at her carton of milk, made a face, and poured the contents down the drain. "I'll lock the door behind me."

When Jason opened the deli drawer and started going through the various packages, Lindsey shook her head and went to shower. The hot water felt wonderful, soothing her aches and pains. She shampooed her hair twice and then was generous with the conditioner, hoping the knots that had inevitably formed during the past few days would be easier to detangle.

Once dry, she slid into long pajama bottoms

and a cotton tank top. She stepped into her slippers and pulled on her short robe, and then, comb in hand, she went to sit on her bed and work on her hair. As she slid the comb through it, she idly wondered what Jason had planned for dinner. She was feeling genuinely hungry for the first time in days.

She was returning the comb to the bathroom when she heard a knock on the door. Her first thought was that Jason had forgotten to take her keys, but as she walked past the kitchen counter, she noted the keys were gone.

Maybe it's Makayla. She opened the door half expecting to see her petite friend.

Instead, a man stood there, and Lindsey found herself staring into a pair of startling blue eyes.

CHAPTER TEN

NATHAN CUT THE engine then gripped the steering wheel with both hands, clenching and unclenching his fingers. He took a deep breath and released it in a rush.

Let's do it, he told himself and slid out of the car. He pulled up the zipper of his leather jacket before shoving his hands deep into the pockets. His breath clouded around him in the cold air.

As he walked along the sidewalk, Nathan tried to match what he saw to the images he carried in his head. Ancient oaks lined the road. Their majestic limbs, now bare, arched over the street that felt a little too narrow even for Nathan's small convertible. The sidewalk was cracked and buckled around the trees' roots. All the buildings appeared to be made of brick. None stood taller than two stories.

After walking half a block, Nathan paused

in front of a single-story duplex. Worrying at the keys in his pocket, Nathan crossed the street and approached the canary-yellow door. He raised his hand but hesitated with it hovering a mere inch from the door. Then, hoping he was not about to make a fool of himself, he knocked.

He quickly shoved his hand back into his pocket; the keys bit into his palm as he waited. When he heard the lock being worked, Nathan looked sharply at the door. It opened, and he caught his breath: Lindsey stood inside the threshold.

He would have known her anywhere.

She looked just as she did in the dreams. She was tall, only a few inches shorter than his own six feet, and slender, but not to the point of being skinny. Her wet auburn hair hung straight over her shoulders and down her back with only a hint of curl at the ends, but Nathan knew that when Lindsey's hair was dry, that hint would become a riotous mass of long, loose curls.

He looked into her jade-green eyes, large against her delicate features.

Too large, he thought, noting the way she stared at him.

He took in her bruised right cheek and the circles under her eyes, and his own eyes narrowed when he realized she was breathing in short strangled gasps, nearly hyperventilating.

"Lindsey?" he asked in concern as she stepped back, letting the door swing open.

She slowly shook her head, and tears welled in her eyes. Her lips barely moved as she murmured, "I'm dreaming. Oh God, I'm still dreaming."

"No, this isn't a dream," Nathan said as he entered the apartment. "No," he repeated emphatically.

When she started to sway where she stood, he stepped in front of her and gently grasped her arms just above her elbows. He bent down and gazed intently into her eyes which were unfocused, fear-filled, and tormented. He questioned whether she still saw him.

"Lindsey, you're not dreaming." He kept his voice calm, but it held a note of urgency. *"I'm here."*

She looked at him in disbelief.

Not breaking eye contact or letting go of her arms, Nathan hooked the door with his foot and kicked it closed behind him. He moved with her, turning them slowly, so that walking backward he led them into the apartment. He looked away from her just long enough to locate a chair.

There was an overstuffed mocha-brown chair to his right, where the hall opened into the living room. He gently urged her to sit then knelt in front of her. Taking her cold and trembling hands in his own, he lifted them to his face, placed them on his cheeks, and held them there.

"I'm here, Linds. I'm *really* here." His tone was steady and sincere as he willed her to believe him. "It's not a dream. I promise."

She leaned forward, and Nathan could feel her breath against his skin. Her eyes searched his.

"Nathan?" she breathed uncertainly, and her hands pressed against his cheeks.

He nodded.

"You're here?" Her voice quavered. "You're r-r-real?"

"Yes and yes." He gave her a small smile. He curled his fingers around hers and lowered their clasped hands to rest in her lap.

Emotions flicked across her features faster than he could decipher. She shuddered as the tension left her body, and she bowed her head.

Nathan bent low, twisted to the side so he could see her face.

Tears ran down her cheeks and fell on their hands.

"Linds, no. It's okay," Nathan said gruffly. He reached up and ran a thumb under her eyes, tenderly wiping away the tears, being careful not to brush against her bruised cheek. He ached to pull her into his lap and hold her as he had done in dreams, but he resisted the urge, fearing she would not welcome his embrace in the waking world, wondering if he had made a mistake in coming to her.

"I'm okay," she mumbled.

"Yeah?"

Lindsey lifted her head, and their eyes met.

"Yeah," she answered, sounding much steadier and smiling. But the smile faded with the sound of her front door opening.

"Jason." She whispered the name and bit her lower lip.

Nathan looked past the chair and saw a man walking toward them, his eyes locked on Nathan.

After a brief glance at Lindsey's worried face, Nathan reluctantly released her hands and stood. He scrutinized Jason's features, hoping to see some family resemblance to Lindsey. There was none. Nathan mentally kicked himself for not considering the possibility that she might be involved with someone.

Standing slightly taller than Nathan, Jason

moved down the hall with the easy confidence and familiarity of someone who knew he belonged there. With a canvas grocery bag hanging off one shoulder and a couple more bags grasped in each hand, he was imposing, instead of safely domesticated.

Without taking his eyes off Nathan, Jason set the bags on the floor. He challenged in a low growl, "Who the hell are you?"

Lindsey got to her feet, and Jason turned his attention to her.

"You've been crying, Linds," he observed and turned accusing eyes to Nathan.

"Jason," Lindsey began warily. "This is Nathan."

Jason stiffened and his lips whitened with tension when he heard Nathan's name: it obviously meant something to him. Nathan wondered what Lindsey had told him.

"Nathan, Jason." Lindsey completed the introduction in a rush, but neither man spoke nor offered his hand to the other.

With his hands fisted at his sides, Jason glared at Nathan, looking like he wanted to take a swing at him.

Lindsey shifted nervously.

Nathan considered Jason's hostility oddly disproportionate for the situation. Uncertain what he had walked into, he chose to remain silent.

"Lindsey, can I talk to you?" Jason ground out through clenched teeth as he brushed past Nathan and grabbed Lindsey's left arm to steer her away.

Nathan's stomach knotted at the casual way Jason took hold of her—touched her—and then he noticed the way she paled and flinched at the contact. He started forward, ready to intervene, but Lindsey caught his eye and subtly shook her head. He held back and unhappily watched the couple disappear into the room at the end of the hall.

Jason shot Nathan one more venomous look before closing the door.

Left alone, Nathan explored the small living room.

Except for the space taken by a fishbowl, the bookcase overflowed with textbooks and paperbacks. Nearly all the textbooks dealt with the sciences: biology was the most prominent. The paperbacks ranged from the classics of Jane Austen and Shakespeare to contemporary science fiction and fantasy authors. Nathan carefully removed a book with the spine so worn the title and author were illegible. He read the cover—*The Blue Sword*, Robin McKinley. Putting the obviously well-loved book back on the shelf, he moved to look at the pile of movies stacked on top of the television. Half listening for Lindsey and Jason to return, he perused the titles and noted several that were favorites of his and in his own collection.

Jason's voice carried down the hall like a thunderous rumble. His words were indistinct but his tone was clearly agitated.

Nathan sighed and raised a hand to work the muscles in his neck. He wandered back to the hall and looked down to the room where Lindsey and Jason were talking. The door was still closed, muffling the conversation on the other side.

For a moment, Nathan considered leaving and contacting Lindsey another time, but the idea felt too much like betrayal, or desertion.

I'm not leaving until Lindsey asks me to.

Nathan shed his jacket and draped it over the chair. He grabbed the canvas bags Jason had put down and took the groceries into the kitchen. One of the bags was loaded with cold foods. Nathan placed that bag by the fridge and started unloading the contents.

With a carton of milk in one hand, he reached for the handle on the refrigerator and paused when he noticed the photographs attached to the door with a bunch of bird-shaped magnets. Jason and Lindsey were together in several of the pictures, too many for Nathan's comfort. There were also photos of a young man who looked too much like Lindsey to be anyone other than her brother. One shot showed Jason with the young man, their arms around each other's shoulders in easy camaraderie.

Trying to set aside his unease, Nathan continued putting the food away.

"Making yourself right at home, aren't you?" Jason snidely asked from behind him.

"Jason," Lindsey hissed.

Nathan turned in time to see her poke Jason as she sidestepped him and walked into the kitchen.

"Thank you." Lindsey gave Nathan a grateful smile. "Have you seen the ibuprofen?"

"No. Not yet." Nathan felt himself relax under her gaze, realizing she wanted him to stay.

He watched as Lindsey got a one-handed grip on one of the bags and, with some effort, lifted it onto the counter near him before starting to rummage through it. Looking over Lindsey's head, he saw Jason scowling at him.

Let him scowl. Nathan dismissed him and turned his attention to Lindsey. She had found the ibuprofen and was struggling with the child-proof lid. Silently, he held out his hand for the bottle. He read the gratitude in her eyes as she gave it to him. He opened the bottle while she got a glass from the cabinet and filled it from the tap.

After Lindsey was done with the sink, Jason slammed a large pot into it and turned on the water. He then went back to putting things away, his frustration evident as he forcefully closed the cabinet doors.

Lindsey returned to Nathan's side and took the open bottle from him. As he finished putting away the food, Nathan surreptitiously watched her pour the pills into her hand, trying to gauge her pain. She started with four, considered them for a moment, and then put two back into the bottle.

Nathan pitched his voice low so Jason could not overhear. "If you need them..."

Lindsey looked at him through her lashes. "It probably would be better if I didn't fall asleep during dinner."

She set the bottle aside with the cap loosely sitting on top and took the pills.

Leaning close to him, she spoke softly, "I'm sorry Jason is being such an ass. He thinks you did this to me." She gestured to her cheek before placing her hand on the counter. "I told him what really happened, but…"

Nathan heard the hurt in her voice and gave her hand a sympathetic squeeze. He could well imagine what it had cost her to confide in Jason.

She met his gaze, and Nathan lost himself in her eyes, feeling an echo of the connection they shared in dreams. He slid his hand so their fingers interlaced and ran his thumb over her soft skin. Her eyes widened imperceptibly. She drew her bottom lip between her teeth, and Nathan followed the motion as she released it and her lips remained slightly parted. She glanced at his mouth then gave him a look that sent his pulse racing. His fingers tightened around hers. He shifted his weight toward her. She raised her chin in silent invitation, and he lowered his head to accept.

The sudden clatter and clank of Jason dropping a pot of water on the stove had the couple straightening before their lips met.

A blush tinged Lindsey's cheeks, but she did not look away from Nathan.

"If I'm going to cook, you need to get out," Jason said abruptly, his tone harsh.

With a sigh Lindsey rolled her eyes. She slipped her hand from Nathan's, giving his pinkie a playful tug before releasing him. He watched the gentle sway of her hips as she walked away from him.

"Be sure to make enough for three," Lindsey called over her shoulder as she left the kitchen. "Nathan's staying for dinner."

Glaring at Nathan, Jason grumbled, "Wonderful."

Buoyed by Lindsey's response—feeling confident that no matter the relationship between Lindsey and Jason, Lindsey was not indifferent to him—Nathan flashed Jason a hard grin.

Nathan then gathered the empty canvas bags, rolling all but one into a bundle and shoving the bundle into the remaining bag. He moved to follow Lindsey out of the kitchen, but Jason stepped in front of him and slapped a loaf of french bread against his chest with enough force to leave an impression of Jason's hand on the bread.

"Why don't you give me a hand," Jason suggested in a tone that brooked no argument.

Looking at Jason, Nathan could see he was spoiling for a fight. Part of Nathan wanted to oblige him. Part of him wanted to find Jason in a dream, stuff him in a wall, and leave him there. But there was Lindsey to consider, so Nathan settled for taking the bread and uttering a nonchalant, "Sure." Nathan looked to Lindsey and held the bags out to her. "Here, Linds."

CHAPTER ELEVEN

LINDSEY REACHED OVER the sink and took the bags from Nathan.

She fumed as she carried them to the hall closet. Jason was being such a...such a...well, such a *guy*. She wanted to strangle him.

Here was Nathan, flesh and blood, clearly not just a dream or a figment of her imagination, and Jason still would not believe she had been hurt in that dream. He insisted on picking at the situation, trying to find something wrong, some plot, as if Lindsey had grabbed some guy off the street for the sole purpose of saying *See, Jason, I'm not nuts.*

She could picture it: *Excuse me, sir, would you mind coming home with me and pretending we've had an ongoing relationship of several years, but only in dreams, because I need to convince one of my best friends I'm not going insane? Oh, and if you're willing, we'll need to hurry. He's going to be back from the store any moment. Okay? Thanks.*

Lindsey yanked open the closet door and shoved the bags inside. She resisted the urge to slam it closed, not wanting to sink to the juvenile fit Jason was exhibiting.

Jason. Lindsey leaned her forehead against the door. If not for Jason, she would have kissed Nathan. Might still be kissing Nathan. Hell, they might be polishing the kitchen floor by now, which was so not her style and would certainly be uncomfortable, if not painful, given her injuries.

With a heavy sigh, she went back to the kitchen. Maybe Jason had a point, and she needed to take things slow. In many ways, Nathan was a stranger, but as she watched him making the garlic bread, she had a hard time convincing herself that was true. His voice, the touch of his hands, his presence: they all felt achingly familiar.

When Nathan looked up from buttering the bread, their eyes met and held. She felt herself grow warm and her pulse become erratic. He gave her a slow sexy grin, revealing a dimple in his left cheek, and she suspected he knew exactly what effect he had on her.

Jason let the dishes clatter on the counter

and gave Lindsey a dark look. "Dinner will be ready soon," he told her then ordered more than asked, "Why don't you sit?"

Lindsey bristled at his curt and commanding tone. She wanted to remind him that this was her home, but a glance at Nathan, who seemed to find something amusing about the situation, had her turning on her heel and stalking to the couch.

Dinner should be a blast, she thought as she tucked her legs under her and absently turned on the television.

Throughout the meal, Lindsey picked at her food; her appetite had vanished shortly after they sat down to eat. Dinner started with Jason positioning himself next to her on the couch, which would have been fine with Lindsey—it would make staring at Nathan that much easier, and she knew she was staring a lot—except that left Nathan to either pull over the heavy chair or sit on the floor at the coffee table.

Seeing him considering his options, she slid onto the floor. He sat opposite her, and Jason sank next to her in a grudging, sluggish way that left her feeling like she had ruined some male dominance display. Before Nathan could take his first bite, Jason fired his opening salvo.

"So, what do you do for a living?" Jason challenged, sounding like a father trying to determine a man's intentions toward his little girl. His clenched hands rested on either side of his plate.

"I paint. I'm an artist," Nathan answered. "I work in oils."

"Really, and how's that working for you?" Jason's voice dripped disdain.

"Quite well, actually," Nathan replied with a note of satisfaction. He spun the spaghetti around his fork. Looking at Lindsey, he continued, "I'm showing some of my work in a gallery downtown."

Lindsey leaned forward. Her eagerness to hear about his work outweighed her determination to provide Jason with no further evidence of how little she knew about Nathan. "What do you paint?"

Jason frowned at either Lindsey's interest or Nathan's apparent success. She was uncertain which bothered him more.

Nathan put down his fork and reached for his glass. He took a drink before answering. "Occasionally, I'll do a portrait, but normally my paintings are surreal or abstract pieces inspired by dreams."

Jason snorted and stabbed at his food, his

fork hitting the plate with a screech. Lindsey pinched him under the table, reminding him of his promise to leave the subject of dreams to her. A subject she had no intention of exploring with him present.

Looking directly at Lindsey, a hint of meanness in his eyes, Jason discharged his next shot. "Nathan, Lindsey couldn't tell me your last name."

Lindsey's stomach knotted and her eyes burned with incipient tears.

"Gower," Nathan spat. Anger burned in his blue eyes, and his knuckles whitened around his glass.

"Jason, please," Lindsey softly implored around the lump in her throat. "Can we just enjoy our dinner?"

A muscle ticked in Jason's jaw. Ferocity covered his face as he turned to Nathan and coldly continued the barrage. "Are you from the area? Have any brothers or sisters? How old are you?" Jason turned his stony gaze to Lindsey as he worked his fork through the spaghetti, wrapping the pasta around it. "I asked Lindsey, but she didn't seem to know."

Jason lifted his fork to his mouth.

Lindsey's eyes fell to her plate. Wishing the floor would open up and swallow her, or better yet swallow Jason, she withdrew from the conversation. If it could truly be called that. It felt more like an inquisition as Jason continued to interrogate Nathan, asking him about himself, asking him if he knew this or that about Lindsey, taking every opportunity to point out how little Nathan and Lindsey knew each other.

Nathan answered the questions with more patience than she would have, although his curt tone failed to conceal his increasing hostility toward Jason. Her only comfort came from stretching her legs under the table and feeling Nathan nudge her until their legs touched. The contact between them, with Nathan occasionally placing a hand on her leg, kept her steady when she really, *really* wanted to stab Jason with her fork and tell him to leave.

With a heavy sigh, she removed the napkin from her lap and dropped it on the table. She glanced at the men's plates and noted in relief that they were both done eating. Without a word to either of them she stood and moved to clear the table.

As if he had been waiting for a signal from her, Nathan was instantly on his feet, gathering the plates and silverware. Reaching for her plate, he looked her in the eye. "I'll take care of this."

She handed him her plate and, appreciating

the way his jeans hugged his body, she watched him walk to the kitchen until Jason stood and blocked her view.

Looking at Jason and his determined expression, Lindsey inwardly groaned: he was going to lecture her again.

Enough.

"Jason, thank you for cooking. I really appreciate it." Lindsey crossed to the chair where Jason and Nathan had left their jackets. She picked up Jason's and shoved it at him. "Thanks for the groceries. I'm sure I didn't give you enough to cover it. Let me know how much I owe you."

"I don't—"

Lindsey ignored him and continued, "I know you have class in the morning, so you really ought to go."

Reluctantly, he pulled on his jacket and took his keys from the pocket. With a parting venomous glance at Nathan, he headed for the door.

Lindsey walked down the hall with him. When they reached the door, he offered her a curt "Good night."

As he reached for the doorknob, she blurted, "You've never had anything but brotherly interest in me. Why have you been acting all macho and possessive?"

"I don't want to see you hurt." He ran a hand through his hair. He looked away and cursed. Looking back at her, worry etched on his face, he continued in a low tone, "Lindsey, you just met him."

"I've known him a long time," she insisted, raising a finger to emphasize her words.

"Before tonight you knew nothing about him." Jason countered, rigidly pointing down the hall.

"Fine. It's true. I admit it." Lindsey's hands clenched at her sides as she spoke in an angry hush, trying to keep her voice from carrying. "Before tonight, I didn't know that he's an artist; that he has a sister; that he's five years older than I am; or any of the minute details you somehow found it your business to ask him about. But..."

Jason opened his mouth to speak, but Lindsey silenced him with a sharp shake of her head and continued, "There's a difference between knowing the minutiae of a person's life and knowing the person. When it comes to Nathan, *I know him.*"

Jason's shoulders slumped in defeat, and he opened the door.

"Jason." Lindsey relented as he crossed the

threshold, trusting he had acted only out of concern for her. "I'll be fine."

She stepped forward. Putting her hands on his shoulders and going up on her tiptoes, she kissed his cheek. She gasped in pain and surprise when he pulled her into a hard hug. He released her just as suddenly as he had grabbed her.

"I'll talk to you tomorrow?" he asked gruffly.

"Yes," she reassured him.

Not meeting her eyes, he nodded. With his hands deep in his pockets and his shoulders hunched against the cold wind, he left.

She slowly closed the door. The click of the latch sounded loud in the sudden silence. She hugged herself with her right arm and walked to the kitchen. Nathan was waiting there for her, his hands braced beside him as he leaned back against the stove.

With a rush of nervousness she thought maybe Jason was right. Maybe this was a bad idea. Nathan really was a stranger.

"Just say the word and I'll go." His words were barely a whisper.

Lindsey looked into his eyes, caught again by the vibrant blue, and read his sincerity in them. She bit the inside of her lip and shook her head.

At her silent reply, the tension left his body. He stepped away from the stove. His eyes never leaving hers, he stopped a couple of feet in front of her.

"You've been favoring your left arm all night. How bad is it?" His voice was gruff with concern.

She lifted her right hand and pulled her robe and the strap of her tank top off her shoulder.

As Nathan stepped closer, Lindsey became acutely aware of how thin her top was and that she wore nothing underneath it. How many times had she worn her pajamas around Jason and thought nothing of it? But having Nathan standing so near, the light picking up a hint of red in his dark brown hair, the scent of him teasing her nose, she felt incredibly exposed. She wondered if he had noticed and felt disappointed when the ugly bruise on her shoulder seemed to be the only thing that concerned him.

His jaw clenched and an emotion she could not identify flickered across his face. "How?"

"I got shot," she replied.

"That's why you fell." His gaze remained fixed on her shoulder.

"You saw?" There was a hint of wonder in

her voice.

He nodded. "But I didn't know what had happened."

She glanced at the bruise and flinched at the purple-blue mottle. "It's worse than when I was skewered."

He looked at her intently. "You were stabbed?"

She nodded.

"When?"

"After you found me in the field. After you left, someone else came and—" She waved her hand and shrugged. She pulled her clothes back up over her left shoulder then lifted her shirt to reveal the yellow-green bruise below her sternum.

He sucked in a breath and lifted a hand to the bruise. He stopped short of touching it, but Lindsey could feel the heat coming from his hand.

He looked at her suddenly. "You said *skewered.*"

"Run through," she confirmed, dropping her shirt. Then, grabbing the collar of her robe, she maneuvered it up and back. She turned her back to him and felt him sweep her hair aside. His fingers grazed her neck as he slid them under her shirt and pulled it down to expose her upper back.

"F—" He bit down on the rest of the word.

She looked over her shoulder at him.

He had gone pale. He moved the shirt again, exposing her left shoulder and the bruising there. "Dammit."

Careful not to touch the bruises, he fixed her shirt and robe.

She turned so she was facing him.

"I'm sorry, Linds. This is my fault." He put a hand to the back of his neck. "I led him right to you."

"Why did you?" she asked. At his stricken look, she rushed to clarify. "No, why did you come to me? Why, after all this time?" A hint of accusation tinged her words. *Why did you let me think you were dead?*

"Partly because of this." Nathan gestured to her shoulder then pinched the bridge of his nose. "Can we sit?"

She nodded, and he stepped aside to let her walk before him. She sank onto the couch, sitting in the corner with her legs folded under her.

He sat on the edge of the couch next to her. He rested his elbows on his knees and buried his face in his hands.

"I'm not sure where to start," he admitted.

He angled his body to face her and braced his arm along the back of the sofa.

He took a deep breath and began. "There have always been things wandering around out there. Phantoms. Shadows. Leftovers from someone else's nightmares, maybe. None of us really know what they are. They could be scary as hell and might hurt you, but they had never inflicted any *real* harm."

Nathan gave her a questioning look, silently asking if she knew what he meant. She nodded in understanding: her own experiences with them were one of the few things she remembered with clarity.

"About six months ago," he continued, "they became more...substantial. They didn't have the same sense of presence you or I have, but there was more to them, and they could leave marks on you, real marks, bruises, if you tangled with one."

Lindsey grabbed a throw pillow and hugged it to herself.

Nathan's eyes grew distant as he spoke. "We started tracking them—Sarah and Zach and I. Tried to figure out what had changed. Sometimes we'd feel someone else nearby, but we could never get close enough to see who it was.

"Then Zach disappeared.

"Sarah and I went to the places where he could usually be found—his version of my diner or your hill—but there was no sign of him. It was when we were in one of his places that we were attacked. It happened so fast." He closed his eyes against the memory.

Lindsey reached up and placed her hand over Nathan's where it rested on the back of the couch. A faint tremor ran through it. He uncurled his fingers and laced them with Lindsey's.

He looked at her with haunted eyes and continued in a tightly controlled voice, "There were a half dozen of them. We might have managed, but another dreamstrider showed up. I thought he had come to help." His fingers tightened around hers. "But...the shades answer to him, Lindsey. He told them to hold me while the cold bastard gutted Sarah like a carp, stood over her while she screamed, and watched her die."

"Are you sure? Are you sure she died?" Lindsey asked in a soft, shaky voice.

Nathan bowed his head. "She didn't wake up, Lindsey. She didn't leave the dream—I know what that looks like, what it feels like—and there's been no sign of her. Or Zach."

"Maybe they stopped dreaming, left the way I did," she suggested without any real hope that she was right.

Raising his head, Nathan smiled at her sadly. He reached out, tucked a strand of her hair behind her ear, and trailed his knuckles along her jaw. "Even when someone stops dreamstriding, you can still find traces of them if you know what to look for..." He watched her warily.

Lindsey met his guarded gaze. She bit her lip as she processed what he had said. *You could have found me in my dreams whenever you wanted, but you didn't. Why?* The question was natural, but Lindsey could not give voice to it.

"How did you get away from him?" she asked instead.

A flicker of relief showed in his eyes before they filled with derision. He laughed without humor. "He let me go. Told the shades, or whatever they are, to release me. He waved his hand, and they faded away. Not that it made any difference—I still couldn't move. I felt just as pinned." Nathan paused, his face puzzled. "He gave me this look, told me good night, then turned his back on me and walked off."

She sat, quietly studying him, uncertain what to say.

"I told the others," he said so softly she barely heard him. "They didn't believe me. They didn't think it was necessary for me to come to you, to..." He hesitated a heartbeat. "...to warn you."

Lindsey felt a twinge of worry at his hesitation: she was certain that he had meant to say something else. But, seeing him so disconsolate and remembering the pain of Jason's scornful disbelief, she sympathized with him and set aside her concern, which seemed trivial when faced with a killer stalking them through their dreams.

She gave their entwined hands a gentle tug, drawing his attention back to her. "What happens now?"

"I don't know," he admitted, sounding beaten. "Try to stay out of his way. Stay safe."

"And I've been doing such a good job of that," Lindsey remarked with a wry smile.

Nathan chuckled. "I'm sorry, Lindsey. I really shouldn't laugh."

"If I can laugh, why shouldn't you?" she countered reasonably.
Feeling chilled, she took her hand from his and pulled on the afghan under his arm. "Excuse me."
He lifted his arm and helped drape the blanket around her back. Nathan froze mid-motion when their eyes met.

Lindsey gazed up at him. He was so tantalizingly close. Impulsively, she leaned forward and brushed her lips against his in a soft kiss. Surprised and embarrassed by her boldness, she pulled back, intending to apologize, but he followed her.

He tunneled his fingers through her hair to the back of her neck and held her tenderly as he deepened the kiss. She raised her right hand to his chest and felt his heart beating a rapid rhythm that matched hers.

They slowly broke apart but still clung to each other.

I could lose myself in this man, Lindsey thought with a mix of fear and amazement as she sat with her forehead resting against Nathan's. It was too much, too fast. She wanted more.

"It's getting late. I should go so you can get some sleep." He sounded like he was trying to convince himself and made no move to leave.

"I'm not planning on going to bed anytime soon. About all I've done for the past few days is sleep. I'll probably put in a movie." She straightened so she could see him. "You could stay."

CHAPTER TWELVE

NATHAN SAT LOW on the sofa. He stared blindly at the television, oblivious to the menu cycling repeatedly on the screen. His thoughts focused on Lindsey.

When he accepted her invitation to stay, he had expected her to ask him questions about where he had been and why he had returned. Although he found himself reluctant to volunteer information, he had been prepared to give her the answers she deserved.

But, for the time being at least, she seemed to be putting aside her questions. One movie turned into two, and not once had their conversation strayed beyond the films or inconsequential topics.

She fell asleep halfway through the second movie. She slept now, curled against him, safely enfolded under his arm. He let his head fall back against the couch and closed his eyes. What was he going to do?

Although he worried over her response to his leaving and returning, part of him wished she would wake up and grill him with the same determination Jason had. Would she understand why he had let her believe he was dead? Would she agree it had been for the best? Or would she see his decision as arrogant and high-handed, as he sometimes did when he looked back on it?

When he had sought out Lindsey in the dream, he had no intention of finding her *here*. Of starting something with her. He had wanted to warn her and to ask for her help. He had not counted on this.

Well, it doesn't matter now. Time for a new plan.

The connection they shared in the dreams had carried over into the waking world with surprising force. Nathan would not willingly walk away from Lindsey again.

He placed a light kiss atop her head, tightened his arm around her then winced at the pins and needles that shot through it. He glanced at the hands of his watch: it was nearly two in the morning. Nothing would be resolved tonight. *I should go home,* he thought.

Moving carefully, he slid his arm from behind her and eased himself off the couch. He looked down at her as he tried to work the feeling back into his arm.

Her brow was furrowed. She appeared far from comfortable with one leg folded under her and the other hanging over the edge of the sofa. Her foot just reached the floor.

Continuing to work his arm, Nathan wandered down the hall to her bedroom. After a moment of blindly running his hand over the wall, he found the light switch. He crossed to the bed and pulled back the covers.

Back in the living room, he pulled the coffee table away from the sofa. Having enough room to maneuver, he leaned low and took her into his arms. Her eyes parted as he lifted her.

"It's okay. I've got you," he murmured, brushing his cheek against her forehead.

Her eyes slid shut. She loosely wrapped her arms around his neck and burrowed into him.

He stood still for a moment, savoring the feel of her in his arms.

As he carried her down the hall, he remembered all the times he had held Lindsey like this in dreams. Sometimes when she was on the edge of sleep. Sometimes battle weary. Sometimes terrified and in need of comfort. Always feeling fragile, as if she would shatter or blow away.

She felt fragile now as he lowered her onto the bed and drew the blankets over her. He stood gazing at her, reluctant to leave. He ran his knuckles across her cheek in a silent goodbye.

Her eyes fluttered open. Her hand came out from under the covers and captured his. She held it tight.

"Stay." She spoke softly but with force.

"Lindsey," he began to protest.

"Please." An edge of fear shone in her eyes. "I feel like I'm dreaming. That you're not really here. Please stay," she implored again, her speech slurred by sleep. "I don't want to be alone."

Nathan's protests fled.

"Let me turn everything off. I'll be right back," he promised, disentangling their hands. He moved swiftly through her small home, locking the door and turning off lights. When he returned to her room, he slid his shoes off and climbed onto the bed next to her.

She turned toward him and sighed. He could barely make out her features in the dim light.

"Thank you," she murmured. Her hand found his in the dark. He clasped it gently then felt her grip slowly loosen as she fell back asleep.

He turned onto his back. He focused on

his breathing, keeping it slow and even until all sense of his body and its position fell away. He waited. He felt the full-body twitch against the sense of falling begin to build. Picturing Lindsey's hill, he envisioned himself there. The sense of falling reached its peak, and he let himself fall away, ride a vertigo wave into the dream realm: he was dreamstriding.

He waited as the world formed around him.

He stood about halfway up Lindsey's hill. As he had every night since she had been shot from the sky, he climbed to the top. He absently rubbed his hand against his hip as he went, trying to rid himself of a sudden itching sensation in his palm. At the top, he looked around.

Lindsey lay amid the long grass, barefoot and in her pajamas. Her body slightly transparent, the blades creating strange shadows through her.

Not dreamstriding, Nathan noted. Still, she appeared closer to that state now than the other nights he had come and stood sentinel.

He lowered himself beside her, balancing on the balls of his feet. He spoke her name softly. When that elicited no response, he sent it silently.

She stirred and her form solidified. Her eyes cracked open to study him blearily. "Nathan? Is it morning already?"

He smiled. "No."

Lindsey looked away from him and took in her surroundings. "Dream?"

"Yeah," Nathan said, pleased she had healed enough to dreamstride again.

Her eyes met his. She raised a hand and touched his cheek. The feather-soft gesture sent a shiver of awareness through him.

"I can still see you," she stated with satisfaction.

"Haven't you always?" he asked, surprised at this revelation.

"No. Not your face." Lindsey stretched, her arms and legs extended to their fullest. She then pushed herself into a reclining position, her arms braced behind her.

"But you've always seemed to recognize me." He shifted to sit cross-legged, facing her.

"I did, but it was more of a feeling like—" Lindsey bit her lip then went on in a rush, "Like sitting in a sun spot on a winter day. Warm and light. I never knew your name before a couple days ago, in the city, and I had only seen your face once before that. The other times, if I could even really look at you, it was blurred." She gazed at him with anxious eyes.

Nathan had a sick feeling that he knew when

that one time had been. He had to ask.

"The one time you saw me...When? When was it?"

Lindsey looked away. She drew her knees up and hugged them to her chest.

"When you...died." She stumbled over the last word.

Nathan hung his head and shut his eyes against the pain in her voice.

"Why?" Her voice shook as she went on. "Why did you let me think you were dead? Do you have any idea what it was like to watch you... to see...and not be able to help or...or stop...or do anything about it?" She drew in a ragged breath.

He focused on the patch of grass coming up between the circle of his legs. He plucked a blade and systematically shredded it.

Four years ago, he had thought only of convincing Lindsey to stop dreamstriding. Whatever pain it may have caused her, at the time he had deemed it worth it. Not until he had helplessly watched Sarah being butchered had he understood what he had done to Lindsey. Only then had he appreciated the trauma he had inflicted upon her with the death scene he had staged.

In retrospect, it was cruel and possibly unforgivable. Nathan felt unable to defend what he had done, but he would do his best to explain his actions.

"What do you remember? From before?" Nathan asked.

"Not much," she admitted, staring into the distance. "Just a sense of always running. Being chased. Being scared...really, really scared." She looked in his direction then quickly looked away again. "I remember you showing up when things got really bad."

"How...how many times would you say you've seen me? Met me in a dream like this?" Nathan waved a hand around. "Not including the last couple of weeks."

"I...I'm not really sure. I feel like you've always been there—here—but if I really think about it...I can only remember five...maybe six times with any kind of clarity, and even those are kind of fuzzy."

Nathan nodded. He suspected as much. Memories of dreamstriding were no different from memories of ordinary dreams: they faded with time. Only frequent dreamstriders seemed to recall their experiences with the same clarity of their waking lives.

"Except for the last time," she added in a brittle voice. "The last time I remember quite clearly. All of it."

Nathan winced. He tipped his back and shifted where he sat in the damp grass.

"When I first met you." He smiled unconsciously at the memory. "You literally ran into me." He brought his hands together. "*Bam.* A full-force collision. Knocked me over." Nathan cast a quick glance at her. She sat with her chin resting on her knees.

"You were up and running again before I could figure out what had happened. The way you took off." Nathan shook his head. "You moved like the hordes of hell were behind you. I started after you. I was kinda pissed and wanted you to know it. I caught up to you and—" He stopped, remembering the way she had burrowed into him, shivered in his arms.

The implicit trust of her embrace and her silent entreaty for help had inspired a deep need to protect her. Nathan had found himself clinging to her just as desperately as she clung to him: their bond formed in that instant.

Nathan shook himself from his reverie. He frowned and started shredding another piece of grass. "Then I saw what you were running from. I'd never seen anything like it. Some bizarre skeletal thing with neon-green hair flying all over the place and this giant yellow handbag with red ducks embroidered on it. At first, it seemed kind of comical," he acknowledged. "But, when it got close...that thing gave off this miasma of everything dark and creepy. Rotten. Evil." He shuddered. "You had good reason to run. I wanted to run."

Lindsey shifted. He caught the movement from the corner of his eye, and he met her steady gaze.

Her eyes held no hint of remembrance.

"You don't remember any of this," he stated, unable to keep his sorrow over her lost memory from filling his voice.

Biting her lip, she shook her head in a short, crisp motion.

He nodded in resignation.

"So, what happened?" she asked softly.

Nathan shrugged. "You teleported us. It didn't follow."

Lindsey's expression was incredulous. "That's it?"

"More or less," he confirmed.

She shot him a disgruntled look. "I get the feeling I'm getting the 'less.'"

"Lindsey, the thing is...Almost every time I saw you, it was like that first time. You were running from something. Scared. Sometimes all beaten up." He turned to her. "You can do more here than anyone else I've met."

She shook her head.

"I never thought to do half the stuff I've seen you do. I *still* can't teleport. But you..." Nathan reached out and tucked a piece of hair behind her ear.

"Some dreamstriders see this place as a giant playground. A place to explore possibilities, to see what we can create and do. There's a thrill in being able to do things that aren't possible when we're awake," he explained quietly, almost feeling a need to apologize for enjoying what so clearly terrified her.

"For all you can do, you never seemed to take any joy in it. Except for flying," he said with a sad smile. He looked away from her and hesitated before continuing. "I talked to some of the others about it—why you would keep coming here. Some of them had met you. They seemed to think..." Nathan paused. His cheeks grew warm. "They seemed to think that you kept dreamstriding because of me. I figured if..." He swallowed hard. "If I wasn't around, if I could convince you I wasn't coming back, if you thought I was dead, then maybe..."

He fell silent. He forced himself to face Lindsey.

She studied him through narrowed eyes.

She started to speak, stopped, and tried again. "Sooo...you faked your death—let me think you were dead—so I would stop...dreamstriding," Lindsey summarized, stumbling over the last word like it was foreign.

Nathan nodded.

"You've got to be kidding," she snarled.

Unable to meet her gaze any longer, he looked away. "I know it sounds...conceited, but—"

"You're right it sounds conceited," Lindsey interjected. "You...you...*idiot!*" She backhanded his upper arm. He grimaced and cast her a quick sideways glance.

"What were you thinking?" she demanded. "Oh, I know what you said. But really? Did that really make sense to you?" Her voice dripped with disdain.

"Yes," he shot back. "At the time, it did."

She groaned. "Why not just, I don't know..." She waved a hand in the air. "Why not tell me to stay away? Tell me to get lost? Why the staged death?"

Nathan looked Lindsey squarely in the eye. He reached out and wrapped a hand around her ankle. She tensed at the contact, started to pull away. Then, her eyes widened as he opened himself to her, laid bare to her his thoughts and emotions.

"I wouldn't have stayed away. Letting you think I was dead was the only way I could think of that would keep me from coming to you." He hoped she could feel his sincerity. "Lindsey, you were..." *Are everything*.

Lindsey's breath hitched.

"The thought of your reaction if I returned...to try to explain *why*." Remorse choked off his voice. *It's been enough to keep me away*. He withdrew his hand.

A tear ran down her cheek.

"Ah, hell, Linds," Nathan muttered. "I'd rather you yell at me than see you cry. You should yell at me."

Her lips quirked into a quick smile. She wiped her hand across her cheeks and started to say something, but she stopped short. Her brow furrowed as she twisted to look over her shoulder.

"Do you feel that?" she asked.

Nathan tensed. "What?"

"Cold." Lindsey got to her feet in a single fluid motion. As she rose, shoes appeared on her feet. Her pajamas changed into snug jeans and a fitted white blouse. Her hair no longer hung loose; instead it was drawn into a tight french braid. Her right hand hovered over a shadow on her thigh, a weapon waiting to be drawn.

It was an effortless, seamless transformation.

Nathan climbed to his feet. He cast out his senses, seeking what had set Lindsey on edge.

There. A cold current flowed through the wind.

Nathan stepped forward, positioning himself next to Lindsey.

She stiffened. "It's him," she hissed.

Nathan darted a quick glance at her.

She held her chin tucked low. Her lip was curled and her nostrils flared. Her eyes focused on an unseen enemy. There was a feral air to her.

"Lindsey," Nathan murmured her name uncertainly.

The space around her began to shimmer.

"Lindsey," he barked urgently. He reached for her.

She took a half step back and disappeared.

His hand passed through emptiness.

"Damn." Nathan raked his hands through his hair. He turned in place, alternately searching for a sense of Lindsey and the murderous dreamstrider.

"Damn," he repeated softly. He rubbed his

itching hand up and down his thigh. Where had she gone?

The temperature dropped.

The sky grew overcast.

"I see she left you behind," a deep voice drawled.

Nathan whirled to face the speaker, willing his sword into his hand as he turned.

A tall man draped in moving shadows tinged with blue stood a dozen paces away. He slowly approached Nathan, the shadows falling away as he neared. "You won't be needing that." He gestured carelessly at Nathan's sword. With an amused smile, he continued, "Not this time, at least."

"Who the hell are you?" Nathan demanded.

"Tsk, tsk." He shook his head. "Names are powerful things. If you know what to do with them. Surely you don't expect me to just give you mine?" He stopped just beyond the tip of Nathan's sword and asked in mock innocence, "Do you...*Nathan?*"

Nathan felt a wave of bitter cold wash over his body. He tried to lunge at the man, run him through, but his muscles locked in place. A great weight pressed at him from all sides. A buzzing filled his ears as he struggled against invisible bonds.

His tormentor laughed and paced around him. "You know, when I fell asleep tonight, I didn't think I would have a chance to..." He stopped and leaned in close then continued with obvious relish, "Play."

This isn't a game, you bastard, Nathan yelled silently. If the man heard him, he gave no indication.

"Imagine my delight to feel Lindsey's return." His eyes took on a thoughtful look. "She is really much more resilient than I thought. I didn't give her enough credit." He looked in the direction that Lindsey had disappeared. "She may be what I need after all." He raised a hand to his mouth and chewed his thumbnail.

Nathan tried again to move.

The man's hand dropped to his side and he shot an irritated look at Nathan. "Give it up, already. You're not going anywhere until I'm ready to let you go." His eyes were lit with anger. "You really disappoint me. After everything I heard, I expected more from you."

Nathan felt cold shock go through him. Who had this man been talking to?

"The only thing you've been good for is flushing out Lindsey." He spocked an eyebrow at Nathan. "Shall we see who can find her first?" he inquired almost pleasantly.

"No," Nathan ground out through his clenched jaw. "Let's settle this. Just us. Leave Lindsey out of it."

"Ha. Oh, that's rich. You've already lost." He grinned maliciously. "Lindsey, on the other hand..."

The man stalked away. The shadows deepened around him, the air shimmered, and he disappeared. The buzzing ceased, the suffocating pressure lifted, and Nathan stumbled at his sudden release.

Dammit, he thought. *Leave it to the psycho to be the only other dreamstrider to have figured out teleporting.*

Nathan focused on Lindsey with renewed urgency. Where would she have gone?

The itching sensation in his hand returned with a vengeance.

What the hell? He raised his hand, looked at it, and froze.

In the palm of his right hand, there was an opalescent mark, oblong with a few darker, irregular areas along its length.

The memory of holding one of Lindsey's bloodied feathers—of watching it dissolve into his hand—rushed back to him. He felt a surge of excitement. He had suspected then they might be bound together. Could it be...? Shutting his eyes, he focused on Lindsey, on the sensation in his hand.

With a sudden, disorienting jerk, he hurtled through the dream realm.

CHAPTER THIRTEEN

LINDSEY FLED.

Only when exhaustion started to overtake her did she stop.

She found herself on a well-maintained path. It was weed-free and its borders clearly defined. The mulch lay thick and spongy beneath her. Tall pines towered over her, casting dappled shadows across the ground. The occasional trill of birdsong sounded.

"Nathan." Lindsey turned toward him. "Do you know where—" The question died in her throat when she realized he was not with her. She spun in a frantic circle. Where was he? Surely he had come with her? When had they become separated?

She thought back.

They had been on the hill—her hill—talking. Then, there had been the cold, and she had known that the man who had taken to hunting her was on the way. She had run away. No, she had teleported.

"Oh, no," Lindsey whispered in a strangled voice. *Nathan can't teleport.* Her hands flew to her face. *I left him behind.*

She swayed then fell to her hands and knees. Her eyes grew heavy.

As she started to lose sense of her surroundings, Lindsey recognized the sensation of slipping out of the dream.

No, she silently chastised herself. *You will not wake up. You will stay here. You will find him.*

Lindsey dug her hands into the mulch. Bits of bark stabbed into her palms, and she welcomed the pain. She used it to ground herself and, with relief, felt the dream solidify around her.

She sat back on her heels. She swallowed down her guilt and fear for Nathan. Could she get back to him? She bit her lip. Probably not.

Fear had driven her from the hill. Instinct had compelled her to race from one location to the next without lingering in any of them. They had passed by in a blurred rush. Without question, Nathan would attempt to follow her, but she doubted she could consciously retrace her path from either direction. If there was any other way to find someone here, it was beyond her knowledge.

Fatigue was another issue; she could feel it gnawing at her. Her hold on the dream could easily slip at any time.

Slowly, she got to her feet. She brushed her hands together, dislodging a few pieces of mulch. Once again, she tried to find some sense of Nathan. There was no hint of his golden warmth, but farther down the path there was a faint niggling sensation of *someone*. Maybe more than one someone.

If she was feeling the others Nathan had told her about, they might be able to help her find him. On the other hand, she could have sworn that she had felt their presences before and that they had avoided her. Would they stay if they felt her coming? Would they listen to her? Would they help?

Lindsey licked her lips and clenched her hands. She had to try. Filled with anxiety, she started down the path.

As she walked, she periodically paused to check for some sign of Nathan. Her hope of finding him dwindled with each failed effort. Her only comfort, small as it was, came from still sensing other dreamstriders ahead of her.

She was about to stop and check yet again

when a low shape appeared along the path. She froze and watched it approach. As it loped closer, the indistinct shadow resolved into a wolf. Large and grey, a hint of rust on his muzzle, he stopped a few feet in front of Lindsey. His ears pricked forward and his head cocked to the side as he regarded her.

Lindsey looked into his golden eyes and recognized him for a dreamstrider; he possessed that strange hyperclear sense of being. To Lindsey, he felt fluid and somehow dark. *But fizzy. Like warm soda.*

"I guess I'm not the only one who shapeshifts," she murmured.

The wolf's jaw fell open and his tongue lolled in a canine grin.

Lindsey returned his grin.

The wolf looked over his shoulder at the way he had come then turned back to Lindsey. She could swear there was amusement in his eyes. He gave a strange yip-snort in apparent laughter then trotted off into the neighboring woodland. He disappeared into the shadows before Lindsey thought to call him back and ask for his help.

"Wait," she cried out, hoping he might hear her. "Please come back." She stared at the last place she had seen him. The shadows remained still, without any hint of his warm fizz. "Damn."

Lindsey cast a pensive look down the trail. What had the wolf found so amusing? With a deep sigh, she shrugged off her misgivings and continued down the path.

As she followed it around a gentle curve, a slight breeze stirred the fine hairs that had escaped her braid. She shuddered as a chill crept up her spine. A shadow moved in her peripheral vision. She froze and cast a wary glance into the woods. A prickling sensation crept across her scalp. She licked her lips and dropped a hand to the blade at her side. Other than the dreamstriders that awaited her farther along the path, she sensed no one else near her. She saw no signs of movement; heard nothing that suggested someone hid in the shadows. She detected nothing that indicated she was anything but alone in this place, but she could not shake the certainty that she was being watched.

Her hand closed around the handle of the blade as she withdrew a step. She pivoted and moved away through the pine needles at a hurried walk, which soon turned into a jog, then full flight, fear nipping at her heels. When she abruptly found herself standing on the edge of a Japanese-style garden, she stumbled to a halt.

Two pale grey stone lanterns marked the entrance. Beyond them, the mulched trail turned into a pebbled path. She crossed into the garden, and her sense of the other dreamstriders sharpened: they were here somewhere. She looked around. A dense, shoulder-height hedge demarcated the garden's boundary. Within it were orderly clusters of plants, all in shades of muted green.

Lindsey followed the path, hoping it would take her to the others. She passed a small sand-and-rock garden off to one side. Its shape lacked the organic, fluid feel she expected; it was rigidly geometric. There were various stone lanterns placed throughout the garden. Despite the space between them, Lindsey felt that the lanterns, too, were arranged in some pattern.

A little way in the distance, she saw a teahouse. Feeling a quick surge of hope that she had found the other dreamstriders, Lindsey quickened her pace and hurried toward it. But as she neared it, she saw that the shoji doors stood open, revealing an interior empty of everything but a low table.

With a frustrated sigh, she cast her senses out, determined to pin down the dreamstriders' whereabouts. Her eyes narrowed and her nostrils flared when she felt them. Focused on the clustered hodgepodge of sensations that signaled the group's presence, Lindsey proceeded through the meticulous grounds.

The path intersected a shallow stream, and a small wooden bridge gracefully arched over it. The sound of the water cascading around the rocks that broke the stream's surface provided a soothing element in the otherwise uptight garden. Fighting the sudden, irrational urge to tromp through the pristine setting and cross the water via the stones or simply jump from bank to bank, Lindsey remained on the path and traversed the bridge. She rounded a bend and stumbled on a scene that provoked a strong sense of déjà vu.

A small group, their eyes shut, sat on the ground forming a circle. In the center floated a miniature sun. The brilliant orange sphere shifted ever so slightly to float from in front of one person to the next. It wobbled occasionally, drawing a frown from an older man sitting directly across from where Lindsey stood.

While she had no clear memory of ever sitting with these people, Lindsey felt certain she had. She was equally certain she had been the recipient of the man's frown before. The sight of it made her nervous to the point of nausea.

Lindsey cautiously approached the group. As she neared, the man's eyes suddenly flew open. He stiffened at the sight of her.

"You," he said.

The small sun flickered, flared, went out.

Everyone turned to look at Lindsey. Their regard ranged from curiosity to fear to hostility. There was no welcome. Some leaned close to each other in whispered exchanges. One woman clutched at the arm of the man next to her; he patted her hand in an absent soothing gesture while he scowled at Lindsey.

A sharp stab of panic pierced her. She scanned the crowd and found the source. When their eyes met, the person flinched and faded away, gone before Lindsey could say if it had been a man or a woman.

Stone-faced, the man who had spoken got to his feet. "You are not welcome here. I told Nathan that."

"Nathan didn't bring me," Lindsey said. "I need—he needs help," she hastily amended, suspecting this man would not help her but might help Nathan.

"Isn't that what *she's* for?" someone whispered as the man continued to glare at her.

"Me? Help Nathan?" Lindsey slowly shook her head. "How?"

The man's eyes narrowed. "An excellent question."

Lindsey shook off her confusion. "Please," she pleaded then grudgingly admitted, "I can't get back to him. I left him with..." She looked away and blinked back tears, not really understanding why but hating that *this* man should see her like this.

"His phantom murderer, no doubt," he muttered.

Lindsey shot him an angry look. "He's not a phantom. He's real. I've faced...seen him. I woke up with bruises."

Her assertion sent a ripple of unease among the group.

The couple who sat clutching each other shared a heated exchange. The man's voice barely carried to Lindsey, his tone scornful: "...dramatic fool, pay her no mind. Lawrence says..."

"Lawrence," one of the women began, with a worried look at him. "Maybe—"

"There is no killer." Lawrence cut her off with asperity.

"But Lawrence, to wake up with bruises?" The woman's voice trembled. She drew her lip between her teeth and turned troubled pale blue eyes to Lindsey. Despite the worry clearly etched on her face, she remained silent.

"This one," Lawrence said, pointing at Lindsey, "is a magnet for trouble. She always has been." Several of the group nodded in agreement.

"Humph."

"Absolutely."

"Too true."

"Remember when..."

"...such a relief when she left."

The group chorused in response, animosity and condemnation reverberating with every utterance.

Lindsey's forehead wrinkled in confusion. What had she walked into? She came to get help. What had she done to provoke such a heated reaction?

"How do I know you?" she asked numbly.

"You don't remember." Lawrence sighed. A muscle jumped in his jaw, and his eyes slid shut as he raised a hand to rub his forehead. "I should have expected as much."

"Ha. She doesn't remember," one of the other men said. "She always was undisciplined," he pronounced haughtily. He looked around at the others in the circle, clearly enjoying being center stage. "She couldn't even control an energy sphere, let alone summon one."

His observation drew a superior snicker from more than one member of the group.

Lindsey barely registered the remark. Her attention centered on the golden warmth taking shape behind her.

"Maybe not," Nathan's voice interjected. "But she can do a lot of other things."

Palpable relief flooded Lindsey. She spun to face Nathan. His face mirrored the relief she felt. She started to apologize for leaving him, but he placed a single finger against her lips, stopping the words before they could form.

The simple contact had the bond between them flaring.

Lindsey shut her eyes at the wave of soothing comfort Nathan sent her. He stepped closer and moved his hand to her neck, wrapping it under her heavy braid. With a ragged sigh, Lindsey closed the distance between them. She wrapped her arms around his waist and buried her face against his chest.

I'm so sorry, she silently apologized.

Nathan held her to him. *Lindsey, hush.* He tempered the gruffness of the thought with a soft kiss on her temple.

"You had to go find her, didn't you." Lawrence's voice intruded.

Nathan slowly disengaged himself from Lindsey's embrace. He stepped forward and confronted Lawrence. "She needed to be warned."

"We both know that isn't the reason you've brought her here." He gave Nathan a meaningful look. "You've been waiting for an excuse to hunt her down for years. Now you've got your phantom killer."

"He's no phantom," Nathan said angrily. "I saw him kill Sarah. He's attacked Lindsey more than once and came after her again tonight."

The group members shifted where they sat and exchanged troubled glances. The woman with the pale blue eyes licked her lips and ran a shaking hand over them. She turned frightened eyes to Lawrence.

"And you stepped in and saved the day, didn't you?" Lawrence's voice dripped with contempt.

"Hardly," Nathan snapped. "I'm helpless against him. He could have killed me more than once. I'm only alive because...I don't know why. Apparently, I disappoint him." Nathan cast a worried glance at Lindsey. "He's focused on someone else."

Lindsey shivered in fear. She stepped next to Nathan and slipped her hand into his. He squeezed it reassuringly, but his eyes revealed his own fear.

"Her?" The man in the circle guffawed.

"She's never had any skill." Lawrence nodded his agreement. "You're the only reason she didn't follow the normal pattern and stop dreamstriding as a child. Look at her. Still clinging to you like the weak little girl she's always been." The man's ridicule tinged the air. "And you thought she'd be able to help you."

Lindsey frowned, confused by this second assertion that Nathan needed her help. She looked to him, but he stared at Lawrence in stony silence. Through their bond, she could feel the emotions roiling through him.

"She's worth more than a hundred of you," Nathan stated flatly, fixing the man in the circle with a contemptuous look.

Lawrence slowly unfolded his arms and let them fall to his sides. Scorn rolled off him in visible waves, obscuring those who sat around him. With deliberate strides he passed through the group and came to stand in front of Nathan. Speaking in low tones that barely reached Lindsey, he said, "You should have left her alone. She can't help you. She *can't* give you what you want."

"You're wrong."

A muscle ticked in Lawrence's jaw. "I won't clean up your mess again." He glanced at Lindsey before turning his back on them and returning to the group.

Lindsey watched him go, wondering if she had correctly read what she had just seen in his eyes. Had it been pity? Why would he pity her?

Nathan turned to Lindsey. *Let's go.*

She let him lead her away.

The muttering of the group followed them.

"Lawrence, if Nathan says—" Lindsey heard the woman with blue eyes begin, only to be cut off by Lawrence once more.

"Relax, Abby. You're safe here, and as for Lindsey, Nathan has *never* thought clearly where she is concerned." Lindsey recoiled at the acid in his tone. Nathan's shoulders tensed and his grip on her hand tightened, but he continued without hesitation.

They wandered back across the bridge and out of the garden. When they reached the mulched trail through the woods, Lindsey drew Nathan to a stop. Still holding her hand, he looked at her questioningly.

She found herself unable to hold his gaze. She struggled with her confusion over Lawrence and the other dreamstriders. She was hurt and frightened by the vehemence of their reaction. The others, though, the way some had cowered…The one who had fled from her as quickly as Lindsey had fled from the murderer…

"Nathan," she started hesitantly. "What did I do to make them so frightened of me?"

Nathan pulled her into a fierce hug. "Nothing," he said grimly. "Absolutely *nothing*."

"Nothing? There has to be something. People don't react like that to nothing." She spoke into his chest.

"Lindsey, I promise you. You've done nothing to Lawrence or his circle." He ran a hand down her braid. "Some of them see you as some type of bogeyman."

"But *why?*" Lindsey wrapped her arms around his waist, leaned into him, and took comfort in his presence. "They don't seem to think I can do much of anything."

Nathan snorted. "That isn't true, and the ones who were dreamstriding when you were here before know it. You're strong and talented. Some of them fear what you can do. I suspect some are also jealous." He kissed her temple. "Lawrence constructed some strict rules for himself and his group. Rules that fit his abilities. You refused to play by his rules.

"I told you some of us like to explore the possibilities. Push the limits. Well, Lawrence— Larry if you want to get under his skin—he's decided we're here to become enlightened. Like this is some plane of higher existence."

Nathan adopted a self-important tone. "'We should work on self-discipline. If we can do things here that we can't when we're awake, it's only to provide us the opportunity to reach beyond ourselves; to gain mastery of ourselves. We should above all resist the temptation to perform unnatural acts. Self-discipline. Self-control. We must constantly strive for both.'"

Lindsey pulled back enough to look at Nathan. "You're kidding."

Nathan shook his head solemnly. "Nope. And he's only gotten stricter in the past few years."

"But what about that floating ball thing? That's not natural. How does that fit into this?"

Nathan shook with laughter.

"What?" She scowled at him.

He cupped her face between his hands. "I was remembering the first time you asked that question." His laughter faded. "That was your first sin in Lawrence's eyes. He was never kind to you after that."

Looking lost in thought, Nathan fell silent. He took a deep breath, and Lindsey could feel him mentally shake himself. There was a subtle shift in his demeanor and his gaze fell to her lips.

"But Nathan," Lindsey protested, trying to ignore the way his thumbs began to trace along her jaw. "It makes no sense. You can't make little, what did he call them, *energy spheres* in the real world."

"I know," Nathan agreed readily as he trailed his thumb over her chin, the pad just brushing against her bottom lip. "What can I say," he murmured, leaning close. "The man's an idiot."

Lindsey made a sound of incoherent agreement against Nathan's lips as he kissed her. She surrendered to sensation. Nathan's lips on hers. His hands running down her back. His body pressed against hers. The bond between them humming with longing. Desire. Need.

With a breathless moan, Lindsey clung to Nathan as her knees went weak. Though he held her firmly to him, she felt herself falling away. With a sharp stab of disappointment Lindsey realized she was losing the dream.

"I'll be there when you wake up," Nathan said.

The thought warmed her but not enough to quiet the insistent sensation that she needed to hold on a little longer, needed to get back and ask Nathan about something Lawrence had said.

CHAPTER FOURTEEN

LINDSEY WOKE TO the sound of running water. Confused, she blinked the sleep out of her eyes and struggled to remember why the water would be on. She peered blearily at the bathroom. The light seeping around the closed door brought the last twenty-four hours back in a rush.

Nathan's here. An unconscious smile graced her lips.

The door opened and light spilled into the room.

Lindsey half raised her hand and squinted against it.

"Sorry," Nathan said, and the light went out.

Momentarily blinded, Lindsey did not see him cross the room, but she felt his weight settle on the bed as he sat next to her. The red spots slowly faded from her eyes.

"What time is it?" she asked.

"A little after five."

Lindsey groaned.

"Not a morning person?" he said, sounding far too energetic.

"It's not morning." She flung a hand at the window. "No sun. It's still night."

Nathan grinned. "I'm sorry. I have a meeting at work this morning, and I need to run home first." In a thoughtful tone he added, "I am glad you're awake, though. I didn't want to leave without letting you know I was going."

"I'm glad you didn't," Lindsey admitted.

After winning a brief fight with the blankets, she sat up, and the two gazed at each other in companionable silence. Before Lindsey could ask him when she would see him again, Nathan spoke, "I would really like to take you to dinner. Or a movie. Or both. Something normal that has nothing to do with dreamstriding."

"I would like that."

"Good." He ran his fingers through her hair, brushing it back from her face. "Why don't you get some more sleep. I'll call you later."

"I'll walk you to the door."

"You don't have to," he protested.

Lindsey shot him a look.

The corner of his mouth twitched. "I'm

sorry. I meant to say, I'd like that." He held out his hand.

Nathan worked the lock when they reached the door. With his hand on the doorknob, he turned to Lindsey, his expression pensive. "Do you remember dreamstriding tonight?"

"Yes," she said neutrally, despite the flurry of emotions the hazy, jumbled memory evoked.

"Good." He sounded satisfied but seemed oddly tense, his expression guarded. "My number's by your phone." He placed a light kiss on her cheek. "I'll talk to you soon." Without waiting for a reply, he opened the door and stepped into the cold.

Lindsey shivered in the crisp late-autumn air and watched Nathan walk down the street. When he was out of sight, she closed the door. After locking it, she drifted down the hall. She found his business card propped against the phone. Scrawled across the back were his cell number and a brief note promising that he would call that night. She flipped the card around again and read the front, which named him as the director of children's programming for the neighboring county's art museum. She set the card on the counter, wondering at his not mentioning his job at the museum last night. The next time she saw him she would ask him about it.

She tried going back to sleep, but her mind was too clouded with thoughts of him and all that had happened.

Giving up on sleep, she sorted through her various assignments, trying to gauge how far behind she had fallen. Throughout the process, images from the dream and snatches of conversation from the past day drifted to the forefront of her thoughts: the words of an anthropology text became meaningless black marks as Jason's voice, drilling her about Nathan, filled her head; a pervading sense of cold fell over her while trying to edit an overdue paper; and she could almost hear Lawrence make a snide comment when in frustration she pushed the paper aside.

After working for a while, but feeling like she had accomplished nothing, Lindsey looked about her. Daylight softly filtered around the curtains. The clock read 7:14.

Slouching against the back of the chair, Lindsey closed her eyes. Calling her mother would have to wait for at least another hour. With effort, she recalled the day. Thursday. One of her lighter days, with only two classes. The first, Shakespeare's Comedies, started at eleven. She had a short half-hour break before Spanish lab but would be free after that. Rooting through a stack of papers, she found her phone and sent a text to Josh to see if he still wanted her help preparing for his biology exam. With no expectation of an immediate reply, she dropped the phone back among the clutter. She glanced at the clock. Only ten minutes had passed.

She sighed and ran a hand up under her hair. It hardly needed washing again so soon, but she needed to clear her head. She knew of no better place to get her thoughts in order than in the shower. Leaving her class materials strewn across her desk, she left the second bedroom that served as her office and headed for the bathroom.

While the water slowly warmed, Lindsey tested her shoulder. She carefully rolled it and winced at the pain. She slowly tried lifting her arm over her head, but she could only bring it to shoulder height. When she wiggled her fingers and touched her thumb to each fingertip in turn, there was no tingling, but when she made a fist and tried to squeeze her fingers tight, her grip still felt weak. Overall, however, her shoulder and arm were better.

Lindsey stuck her hand under the spray of water. Finding it a comfortable temperature, she shed her pajamas. With a soft moan of pleasure, she stepped under the hot stream and lowered herself into the bathtub. She sat with her forehead resting on her bent knees, her arms wrapped around her legs. The water poured around her, a welcome, soothing warmth that relaxed her body and set her mind free to tackle what troubled her.

Nathan.

Jason.

The dreams. The nightmares. Dreamstriding. Whatever you chose to call it.

They all vied for her attention.

Strangely, thoughts of Jason proved the most disturbing. His behavior around Nathan was so uncharacteristically possessive—almost jealous—she found herself starting to rethink their relationship. Had she missed something? She considered him her best friend, practically a brother. Until yesterday, she would have said he felt the same. But now? She hoped his behavior was a reaction to seeing her bruised and battered, prompted by worry and concern for a childhood friend and nothing more. She needed their relationship to stay the same. She needed the security and stability he had come to represent over the years, especially now with the nightmares and Nathan returning.

A drop of water seeped through the curtain of her hair. It traced a path down her cheek to the tip of her nose where it hung suspended until she moved just enough to brush it against her knee.

Thinking about Nathan brought a smile to her lips. Being with him, she felt lighter somehow; the worries of the world melted away when he was near. And yet...Her smile faded. She drew her bottom lip between her teeth.

She believed that he had been truthful with her, but there was something there, a sense that he was concealing something from her. Lindsey set aside pursuing that gut feeling, choosing instead to reflect on Nathan's reason for leaving. On that score, her feelings were mixed.

He had said it sounded conceited.

Arrogant or overbearing would also be appropriate.

Anger simmered with the memory of watching him die, seeing him standing before her one minute then suddenly having one of the many nightmares appear behind him. What the figment looked like, she could no longer recall; its appearance mattered little to her then, or now, and was lost like so many of her experiences during the dreams of her childhood. Nathan, however, in those final moments—that image was forever etched within her mind. The flash of a blade arcing over his shoulder then driving into his chest; blood flowing from the wound; the sorrow and pain in his eyes; the unmistakable feeling he was saying farewell as he disappeared from the dream. Through it all, she stood unable to reach him, unable to help, incapable of even screaming out her horror as a great well of despair rose within her and squeezed her from the dream moments after he faded from sight.

Lindsey drew in a shuddering breath. She screwed her eyes tight against the tears that threatened to fall as they had four years ago when she had woken with the unshakable conviction that Nathan was dead.

Unquestionably, he believed that he had acted in her best interest. It was hard not to be moved by his determination to protect her. It was hard not to be touched by his efforts to shield her from the horrors she had faced in the nightmares, no matter how extreme his methods. But without Nathan's presence overwhelming her, overshadowing her doubts, and filling her with a giddy joy at his return, Lindsey ached.

His return soothed some of the hurt. How could it not? He risked her censure in order to warn her when he believed she was in danger. However, his return also contributed to her pain; he could have found her in dreams at any time. How he had come to be on her doorstep was an entirely different question. Could he have done that at any time as well?

She raised her head, tilting it to let the water push her hair back. She imagined opening the door at age sixteen and finding him there.

Let's see, when I was sixteen, he would have been... Lindsey grimaced and uttered a strained burst of laughter. *Twenty-one. My parents would have had a fit.* She shivered as the water cooled. With a weary sigh, she stood and quickly washed her hair.

Her mind returned to the most recent dream, to the Japanese garden, to Lawrence and the others. There would be no help from that quarter. Had Nathan known what kind of reception awaited her among them? Lindsey shuddered as she turned off the water, stepped out of the shower, and wrapped herself in a towel. She suspected Lawrence would stand by and watch her be killed without lifting a finger to help. He might even celebrate her permanent exit from the dream realm. What he and his circle had said about her lack of control and clinging to Nathan had struck a nerve. Their assessment of her capabilities felt more accurate than Nathan's. There had been something else, something about Nathan. It had troubled her at the time and she meant to ask him about it. She bit her lip, struggling to recall what Lawrence had said, but the memory evaded her.

With a heavy sigh, Lindsey squeezed the water from her hair before reaching for her comb and dragging it through the still-dripping mass. At the sound of her front door opening and closing, a cold, prickling sensation worked its way up her back and over her scalp.

She abandoned the towel for her bathrobe. She wrapped it around her trembling body and tied the belt with shaking hands then paused in the bathroom doorway.

Seeing no one in the hall, she bolted to her nightstand. She grabbed the cordless phone from its cradle and punched in 911. Her thumb hovered over the call button as she crept to the bedroom door. Cautiously, she peered down the hall again. Jason stood at the kitchen counter, Nathan's business card in his hand.

"*Jason,*" she barked as she cleared the call field, and felt a sense of grim satisfaction at seeing him jump. She strode down the hall. "You know, when I gave you a key it was in case I lost mine. Or I locked myself out. Or for an emergency. Not so you could just let yourself in. Did you even knock?" She plucked the card from his fingers. "What if I wasn't alone?"

Jason looked at her steadily. "Then I would have been very disappointed in you."

Lindsey sucked in a breath, feeling like he had just slapped her. "Get out," she said evenly and pointed to the door. Her body trembled with hurt and outrage.

"*You don't know him.*" Dark emotions clouded Jason's eyes.

"I'm not doing this again. Get out." Her nails dug into her palms.

"You just met him."

"I've known him for years," Lindsey insisted, her voice a low growl.

"From dreams?" Jason spread his arms wide as he leaned toward her.

"*Yes,*" Lindsey yelled with enough force to make her throat ache.

Jason raked his hands through his hair and clasped them behind his neck. "Fine," he bit out then continued in a rational tone, "fine. Let's say you met him in dreams. How do you know that he's really the person you dreamed? How do you know that how he appears in dreams is who he really is?"

"You can't lie about who you are in dreams," she stated with conviction.

"Really? It seems like the perfect place to

be someone else." Jason moved close to her, invading her space, forcing her to retreat. His eyes were intent, probing. In a low, gruff voice he pushed her. "Tell me, Lindsey, when you dream, are you always a college student? Are you going to class? Are *you* who you are now?"

"Not always," she reluctantly conceded in a small voice.

He stepped back. A light of triumph sparked in his eyes.

Lindsey shook her head slowly. "Jason, I may not always be just a bio major in my dreams. I may do things that I can't do here, but the core of who I am doesn't change. I have to believe it's the same for him." She paused. "I trust him."

Jason silently considered her. Drawing a deep breath, he said, "Why now? Did you ask him?" He stepped close to Lindsey. A hint of desperation colored his voice. "Why now? Why is he *here? Now?*"

Lindsey bit her lower lip. She broke away from Jason's acute gaze. The doubts and questions she had set aside in the shower returned full force. She would not confess them to him, however.

"Lindsey," he pleaded, resting his hands on her shoulders.

Unmindful of the pain it caused, she shrugged off his hands and turned away from him. Biting her lip, she struggled for control.

"Why are you doing this?" she asked in a broken whisper. "Is this jealousy? Have I been wrong about our relationship?" Lindsey silently willed him to say no.

"No." His flat denial came after a pregnant pause. It sounded hollow and lacked conviction.

Ignoring the sick, sinking sensation his delayed response triggered, Lindsey chose to take him at his word. "Then why can't you just trust me if not him?"

"I do trust you," Jason said with quiet simplicity.

She snorted in disbelief and angrily brushed away a tear.

"I don't want to see you get hurt. This isn't like you." Jason started pacing in the small space. "You've rarely dated, but when you have, you've taken things slow. The only time I've known you to rush into something was with Robert Dunn." Jason snarled the name. "That was a disaster. I don't ever want to see you that torn up again." He raked a hand through his hair. "I always figured the only reason you'd gotten involved with that creep was because we'd just lost Mike."

Lost in thoughts of the events of four years

prior, Lindsey watched Jason resume his prowling back and forth.

"It wasn't just losing Mike." The softly spoken words escaped her.

Jason stopped and looked at her.

"It wasn't just losing Mike," she repeated. "It was losing Nathan, too. If I hadn't thought Nathan was dead, I wouldn't have gone out with Rob." *Or anyone else.* The bond she shared with Nathan was strong enough that she would have continued hoping to find him someday and passed on every other man who showed interest in her.

"You didn't say anything." Jason's features reflected his confusion.

"What was I supposed to say? That the man of my dreams had just died?"

Jason looked dumbfounded.

"Yeah. Exactly." Lindsey cringed inwardly at the bitterness in her voice. "Dear God, Jason. You've met him, and you still don't believe me. What would you have said, then? Can you honestly say you wouldn't have chalked it up to grief? Or dismissed him as a teenage fantasy? Can you?" Her voice rang through the apartment.

Jason sank onto the couch. With his elbows braced on his knees, he buried his face in his hands. Silently, Lindsey settled next to him and unconsciously mirrored his posture. She remained stern and did not look at him.

"You have to stop this." Her hands muffled her voice. "Nathan's important to me. I don't know what having him in my life will mean. There are things I still need to talk to him about. I know that." She lowered her hands, folding them in her lap. "You have to leave me alone. Let me figure this out by myself." She turned and met Jason's troubled gaze.

"I'm sorry, Linds," he said, clearly sincere and oddly sorrowful. Silence fell between them, and for the first time in the long years they had known each other, Lindsey found it awkward and begging to be filled with words, no matter how meaningless. She shifted in her seat.

Jason cleared his throat. "My gig is this Saturday. Are you still coming?"

"I'll be there," she said, striving for normalcy.

He looked down. "You could bring Nathan."

Lindsey recognized the suggestion as a peace offering. "I'll mention it to him."

"I'll see you then." Jason got to his feet.

Lindsey started to rise, but he waved her back down.

"I let myself in. I'll let myself out." He smiled wryly.

She watched his retreating back, knowing that as much as she wanted it to be otherwise, something had changed between them. She ached at the fracture in their friendship and wondered if it could ever be the same. She heard the door open and close, followed by the faint click of the lock being slid into place.

Numbing exhaustion settled over her, choking coherent thought. She sat on the couch as the shadows slowly shifted, stretched, and changed shape. The faint, distant sound of her phone signaling a new text message roused her. She forced herself off the sofa, found her phone, and read Josh's eager acceptance of her offer to meet later. She sent a quick confirmation. Submerging all thoughts of Nathan, Jason, and dreams, she sought refuge in the day's routine and obligations.

CHAPTER FIFTEEN

TAKING A FRESH canvas from the pile in the corner, Nathan walked to his easel. He maneuvered the small, wheeled workbench to his side, and grabbed a steel can off the bottom shelf and removed the lid.

The distinct smell of paint thinner assailed him.

Reflexively, he inhaled deeply. The stuff might be toxic and he might pay for his choice of materials someday, but he found the smell every bit as good as fresh-baked brownies. Some of the tension drained from him.

Nathan opened the top drawer of the workbench and removed a favored brush. With it in hand, he faced the blank canvas. He shifted his weight from one foot to the other, ran his free hand through his hair, and grasped his neck, waiting for inspiration to strike. Nothing. Nada.

Zilch.

Damn. He had no idea what to paint. The only image that sprang to mind was Lindsey, her green eyes clouded with questions.

Nathan's eyes flicked to a collection of finished work lined up against the wall. He put the brush back in the drawer and returned the lid to the can of paint thinner. With slow steps he approached the canvases. After a moment of hesitation, he shuffled through them and carefully pulled one to the front. He took a step back, sliding his hands into his back pockets.

Lindsey looked back at him from the canvas, captured in the final moment of transformation from hawk to human—her bare toes just shy of the ground, her arms curved out behind her, feathers mingling with her hair.

He had painted it two years ago as a remembrance of her. He had been unable to part with it despite more than one offer to purchase it.

Nathan reached out a hand and ran his fingertips over her cheek. "I need you to remember." His brow furrowed. "I need you to dreamstride."

For the past two nights, he had searched for her while dreamstriding. He had been to her hill and had looked along paths she used to travel. He had even approached Lawrence's group. Little good that had done him. There had been no sign of her, no evidence of her passing through.

He had tried repeating the hand thing. He had focused on Lindsey and waited for the itching to start in his palm. He had been braced for the pull that had occurred before, but nothing had happened.

"Might have been a one-shot deal." Nathan studied his palm. Held just right in the early-morning light, the mark showed faintly. No, not likely a one-off. He closed his fingers around the mark and looked back at the painting.

On his own, he stood no chance at stopping the murderous dreamstrider. The knowledge rankled, but it remained the hard, unpalatable truth. Lindsey, however, he felt certain had the skills, if she could remember them. Dreamstriding seemed the most likely way to trigger her memories. "And the sooner, the better." When he had stopped dreamstriding last night and fallen into true sleep, Nathan had had a dream that made him question the safety to be found even in normal dreams.

He opened his eyes then squeezed them tight and blinked rapidly, trying to bring his surroundings into focus. He was still in bed. He lay on his side with Lind-

sey nestled against him. She was on her back, his arm draped across her waist. She breathed the slow, even pattern of deep sleep.

He let his gaze drift across the room, trying to discover what had woken him. The room was his with a few changes. Red velvet drapes tied back with gold cords hung from a canopy. The walls were wood paneled and stained a dark cherry. A couple of wingback chairs sat in front of the fireplace that occupied the wall directly before him. Swords hung over the mantel. The brackets where his sword normally hung were empty. That blade would be by the bed in easy reach.

Movement in one of the chairs drew his attention. A man rose from it. A cold prickling sensation stole over Nathan as he recognized him. It was the murderer. He slanted a look at Nathan then turned his attention to his hands. He held a dagger and was running it under his nails as he rounded the chair and approached the bed.

Nathan started to reach for his weapon but moved no more than a centimeter when his body froze. A buzzing filled his ears. He felt like a great weight settled over him or that someone had grabbed him by the neck the way a lioness carried her cubs.

"Awake, I see," the man said as he stopped by the bed. Then he held out his hand, fingers spread, nails up. He turned his hand over, curling the tips of his fingers so he could still see his nails, as if inspecting a manicure.

He rubbed his thumb and fingertips together, lowered his hand, and turned his attention to Nathan.

Nathan continued to struggle. He felt his muscles bunch and tighten, but his limbs refused to move. He ground his teeth together in frustration then watched in horror as the man lowered the dagger's point to Lindsey's shoulder, trailing it across the vivid bruise.

"Remarkable," the man murmured. "I'm usually a better shot." Using the dagger, he lifted the sheet, drew it down, and blithely flipped it over Nathan's arm, leaving Lindsey exposed from the waist up. Looking directly at Nathan, he traced the outer curve of her breast with the flat of the blade. "She really is quite lovely, isn't she."

Nathan threw himself against his invisible bonds, wanting nothing more than to kill the bastard. Sweat formed on his brow, but nothing else happened.

The man grinned smugly and looked back at Lindsey. His smile faded as he tapped the blade against the faded yellow bruise below her sternum. He lifted the blade and settled it above her heart, angling it so the blade would slide neatly between her ribs. He squared his stance by the bed and wrapped his other hand around the hilt, getting it in a firm two-handed grip. He leaned over Lindsey and met Nathan's horrified gaze.

"Third time's the charm," he sneered. Then he drove the dagger home.

"Lindsey!" Nathan yelled as he sat up in bed. He turned to the empty space next to him, expecting to see her there. Breathing hard, he ran his hand over where she should have been and struggled with his confusion at not finding her. Running shaking hands through his hair, he fell back onto the cold, damp sheets.

A dream. Just a dream. Not dreamstriding. It had only been a dream. Hadn't it? Lindsey had only been an image? Swallowing hard, Nathan forced himself to replay the dream. Lindsey had lacked the sense of presence that identified a dreamstrider; so had the psycho. So, yes, just a dream.

Still, the buzzing and the pressure. Had it been merely memory at work? Or had it been more? When Nathan dreamstrided, he could find people in ordinary dreams. It took a great deal of effort, but it could be done. Did the murderer also possess the ability? Had he found Nathan and manipulated the dream?

Nathan pulled his hands from his pockets, laced them behind his neck. Even now, hours later, he could not shake his unease, his stomach an unpleasant knot. He would have liked to pass it off as anxiety about seeing Lindsey and meeting her friends at Jason's gig later, but he knew better.

Nathan turned his back on the painting. He

returned to the fresh canvas and once again readied his supplies. Brush in hand, he stood in front of the blank canvas and forced himself to remember Sarah's death: to remember the face of her killer as he stood over her.

He grabbed a tube of paint and squeezed a generous amount onto the palette. The paint looked solid as it came out of the tube, but when the brush sank into it, it almost collapsed on itself like buttercream icing. He worked the brush through it, loading it with the thick oil paint.

The first stroke was always difficult, marring the pristine white surface, especially with a bold color like the deep red on his brush. He purposefully ran the brush across the surface, leaving a trail of pigment in an angry slash. He let his brain disconnect and his hand move freely until the white had disappeared under an uneven layer of red.

Nathan swirled the brush through the turpentine. Gently, he worked the bristles across the wire mesh at the bottom of the old soup can. Meditatively, he pressed the brush against the side, working out the excess thinner before running the brush across a paper towel, leaving faint red trails. With a fresh paper towel, he squeezed more out of the bristles before sinking the brush into the next color. Black this time.

With deft touches Nathan ran the pigment across the canvas, mingling it with the red. Shapes began to emerge.

Nathan worked until he felt a headache setting in from squinting in the increasingly low light. He looked at the clock sitting on a workbench near the window and read the time through the paint-stained display.

"Damn. I'm going to be late."

He hurriedly cleaned his brush and capped the can of paint thinner. Taking one of the paper towels he had been using, he ran it over his hands to remove a couple of smudges then headed upstairs to shower.

CHAPTER SIXTEEN

LINDSEY HASTILY YANKED an emerald-green sweater down over her head then muttered a curse as her sleeves bunched inside it. She struggled to straighten them and eyed the clock. It was nearly seven. *Damn.* Jason and Makayla would be arriving any minute to take her to Dave's with them. She hurried into the bathroom.

Other than some mascara and a touch of gloss, she chose to forgo makeup. Early attempts to conceal the fading bruise on her cheek had made it obvious that nothing short of caking on foundation would hide the blue-green mark.

She grabbed her brush and worked it through her hair, growling in frustration as static simultaneously plastered her hair to her scalp and sent it flying in weightless defiance.

She shot it a look of disgust then pinned it back with a couple of clips. Taking a step back, Lindsey eyed herself critically in the mirror.

"Ugh," she groaned. The sweater had the unfortunate effect of not only bringing out the green of her eyes but the green of the bruise as well.

Snatching the clips from her hair, Lindsey returned to her bedroom. She studied the clothes strewn across her bed. Chewing on her bottom lip and tapping her foot, she debated between wearing one of the previous four outfits she had tried or heading to the closet and starting over. She yanked her sweater off and added it to the pile on the bed.

A knock on the door stayed her hand as she reached for the buttons of the cream blouse. A quick glance at the clock showed it was a few minutes past seven. With a sigh of resignation, Lindsey ran a hand around the waist of her jeans, checking that her blouse was neatly tucked in, and yelled down the hall, "*Come in.*"

"Linds?" Jason's voice reached her.

"In a minute," she replied on her way back to the bathroom.

She dug through a drawer until she found a pair of hair sticks. After twisting her hair into a neat knot, she slid the black sticks into it. She turned her head to either side. "Better."

She selected a simple pair of pearl earrings from a glass dish sitting on the vanity. Now, where had she left her boots? The closet! They were in the closet.

"*Hey, Lindsey?*" Jason yelled.

"Yeah?" Lindsey shoved a small pile of dirty laundry out of the way and retrieved her shoes. Balancing on one foot, she slid the other into a knee-high boot.

"Did you invite Nathan?"

Lindsey stopped midway through zipping the boot.

"Yes," she called over her shoulder, "yes, I did." When Jason said nothing in response, she finished with her boots and donned a russet-colored fitted jacket. Rubbing damp palms against her jeans, she scanned the room, a vague feeling of forgetting something teasing at her. With a shrug and a sigh, Lindsey went to greet Jason.

He stood leaning against the counter, idly tossing his keys while he waited. He stilled and his eyes moved over her in a sweeping glance as she walked in.

Lindsey's stomach tightened at his warm perusal. She licked her lips and snatched her purse off the counter. She clutched it to her, a feeble shield against what she saw in Jason's eyes.

"You look really nice, Lindsey," he complimented her in a husky voice.

"Thank you," she choked out.

Jason made no reply. He simply stood, staring.

Lindsey's heart pounded.

"Should we go?" she prompted with false brightness.

Jason blinked and roused himself.

"Yeah, of course. We wouldn't want to be late." An edge in his tone belied the mildness of his response. He preceded Lindsey down the hall. The click of her three-inch heels sounded around them. When she stopped to lock up, he went ahead to his car. Lindsey watched his retreating back.

"This is a mistake," she muttered softly. "I shouldn't have invited Nathan." After a quick glance at the porch light to make sure it was on, Lindsey threw the bolt. *Maybe I should give Nathan a quick call, explain the situation, and reschedule.*

The sound of Jason forcefully closing the car door caused her to flinch. She cast a wary glance at his silhouette. The street and dash lights created odd shadows over his features. Maybe she was being selfish, but no, she would not call Nathan. Inviting him had been Jason's idea. He would have to live with it. Carefully placing her feet to avoid catching her heels in a crack or sinking them into the ground, Lindsey moved to join Jason and Makayla.

She got out of the car as Lindsey approached. "Hey there, girl. Long time no see. Where have you been keeping yourself?" Makayla said, her broad smile visible in the glare of the street lights. "I can't remember the last time we went for over a week without seeing each other. Jason says you've been sick." With her arms outstretched, she approached Lindsey. "That must have been some bug to keep you—" Makayla stumbled to a halt. Her wide-eyed gaze fixed on Lindsey's cheek as she softly finished, "From class. If you'd called, I'd have come over. To help." She raised one well-shaped eyebrow.

"I'm doing much better now," Lindsey reassured her.

After a searching look and a crisp nod, Makayla said, "Right." She reached up and pulled Lindsey into a quick hug before stepping back to let her into the car.

While Lindsey silently blessed Makayla for not asking about the bruise, she found herself wishing for the steady stream of chatter she could usually count on when in Makayla's company. Without the normal prattle, there was no masking the palpable tension between Lindsey and Jason. Instead, after a few remarks that had provoked no response from either of her friends, Makayla had fallen silent.

Lindsey intercepted Makayla's quick, worried glances. With a slight shake of her head, she advised Makayla not to pursue the matter and offered a weak smile in apology for the uncomfortable situation. Makayla shot her a dark look that promised they would talk later then shifted in her seat to stare out the window.

Jason drove on in stony silence.

When they reached Dave's Dive, Lindsey anxiously searched the room for Nathan. Despite knowing that it was too early and that he was unlikely to be there, she felt a sharp stab of disappointment when she failed to find him.

"Not here," Jason muttered.

"No," Lindsey agreed.

"If they don't get here soon, we're not going to start on time," Jason said.

Lindsey glanced at him in confusion before realizing he meant the rest of the band. She felt her cheeks pinken at her error.

Jason continued to look around the interior of Dave's as if his intense scrutiny could make his bandmates appear. He shifted the strap of the gig bag that hung over his shoulder and tapped the pedal tuner in his other hand against his thigh.

"Well, come on then," Makayla said. "Let's find a place to sit. I'm sure they'll be here soon."

Lindsey and Jason trailed after her as she led them across the worn pine floors, weaving between the hodgepodge of frat house and dorm room castoffs that filled the small space. She stopped at a table with a clear view of the low platform that served as a stage for musical performances and karaoke nights.

Jason put down his gear and dropped his jacket over the back of a chair. "I'm going to talk to Dave. Let him know I'm here. See if he's heard from the guys. Do you want anything from the bar?"

"Diet cola, please," Makayla requested. "Oh, and some onion rings?"

"Sure. Lindsey?"

"Water, please."

"Got it." Jason strode away.

Makayla watched him leave then turned her sharp gaze to Lindsey. "Okay, spill. You drop off the face of the earth for a week then turn up looking like this." Her eyes darted to Lindsey's cheek, and she frowned. "You and Jason are clearly on the outs. What the hell is going on, Linds?"

Lindsey looked away from her friend's scrutiny. Could she tell Makayla? Would she believe her? Or would she be like Jason?

"Lindsey?" Makayla entreated, her voice heavy with concern.

Lindsey met her sympathetic gaze. "Makayla, I—"

"Your drinks, ladies," Jason's voice intruded. He set the cold glasses in front of them. "Your onion rings will be ready in a few minutes." He sat down and took a swig from his beer.

"Thanks," Makayla muttered with an irritated look at Jason.

Lindsey shifted in her chair and crossed her arms in front of her.

Jason took a slow drink and regarded Makayla. "Did I interrupt something?" He looked down at the bottle. "Was Lindsey telling you about Nathan?" His tone had a forced casualness.

Makayla's eyes widened. "Nathan?"

"Lindsey has a date," Jason said and stared into the middle distance with his jaw clenched. His fingers drummed on the table.

"Really?" Makayla drawled. With narrowed eyes she looked at Jason with sudden understanding. She pinned Lindsey with a speculative look.

"Yes," Lindsey admitted, feeling like a canary trapped within the cat's sight. A feeling that only grew with the slow grin that curled Makayla's lips. "His name's Nathan. He's an artist. He works at the art museum," she blurted out in a rush. "He should be here soon. It was Jason's idea to invite him tonight," she added with a defensive note. Her eyes darted to the door. With relief, she spied Jason's band, burdened with equipment, making their way into Dave's. She flashed her friends an overly bright smile. "Oh, look, the guys are here."

Jason raised a hand, signaling his bandmates. They acknowledged him with a couple of waves and a nod of the head.

Makayla's attention remained fixed on Lindsey. "Mm-hmm," she purred. "I have just one question for you." She leaned across the table. It wobbled under her weight. With a wicked grin she asked, "Did you shave your legs?"

Lindsey's cheeks grew hot.

Jason looked between the two women in confusion. "I don't follow."

With a throaty laugh, Makayla explained, "It's winter. The only reason to bother shaving her legs is if she thinks someone may be..."

"Makayla!" Lindsey hissed.

"...feeling them," Makayla finished with relish.

"Can I feel Lindsey's legs?"

Lindsey cringed. She looked up to see Charles, the band's vocalist, grinning at her.

Jason looked down at the table. His hand tightened around the beer bottle in a white-knuckled grip.

Lindsey watched Makayla's good humor fade as she studied Jason's reaction to the conversation. Her eyes held a flash of pain when she looked back to Lindsey.

"Judging from Lindsey's blush, I think it's a safe bet she shaved her legs today." Makayla took a sip of her soda and directed a cool look at Jason. "He must be some guy, Lindsey. I can't wait to meet him." Her bright tone held a brittle, bitter note.

The chair made a harsh squeal as Jason pushed back from the table. He set the bottle down with a thunk. "I've got to set up," he muttered, grabbing his gig bag and the tuner.

Charles dropped into the chair Jason vacated. He picked up the abandoned bottle, studied it, and took a sip.

With a dull ache in her stomach, Lindsey watched Jason walk away to join the rest of the band. She turned to Makayla, who wore a sullen expression.

"Makayla, please, don't make this harder," Lindsey pleaded. "Jason doesn't want me seeing Nathan."

"Of course not, he's not going to approve of anyone you see. He wants you for himself." Makayla cast a dejected look at Jason.

"That's not true," Lindsey said heatedly.

Charles snorted.

"You keep out of this," Lindsey snapped. "Shouldn't you be over there helping them?"

Charles gave her a look of wide-eyed innocence.

"Oh, please, Lindsey." Makayla slapped a hand on the table, causing people at neighboring tables to look at them. She leaned forward and lowered her voice before continuing, "You saw the way he reacted."

Charles nodded sagely.

"Yes, but..." Lindsey shook her head. In a level voice, she explained, "Makayla, Jason thinks Nathan hit me." She pointed to her cheek. "That he did this."

"Did he?" Charles asked with an edge in his voice. He studied her over the rims of his glasses, the look in his eyes sharp and serious.

Makayla waved aside the idea. "Lindsey wouldn't have anything to do with a guy like that. Not that you couldn't get duped by someone, but you'd never keep him around and give him the chance to do it again."

Lindsey felt a surge of warmth at her friend's confident assertion. "Thanks, Makayla." She turned to Charles. "Nathan didn't hit me."

His steady gaze rested on her a moment longer. Then he nodded. He tossed back the rest of Jason's beer before gesturing to the door with the bottle. "And would that be your Nathan there?"

"Where?" Makayla twisted in her seat.

"Over by the door." Charles set the empty bottle on the table.

Lindsey looked past Makayla to the entrance, where Nathan stood with his leather jacket slung over his shoulder. Lindsey cast a quick glance at Charles. "How'd you know?"

Charles shrugged. "Haven't seen him before. And he's obviously looking for someone."

"Guy in the blue shirt? Black jeans?" Makayla asked.

"Yeah," Lindsey confirmed as she got to her feet. Her legs felt wobbly. Nathan's eyes met hers and a warm smile lit his face. Lindsey's pulse quickened as she returned his smile.

"Oh my God! Lindsey!" Makayla squealed. "You're dating a god."

"Jason's screwed," Charles opined.

Lindsey watched Nathan cross the room. His eyes never left her. She hastily ran her hands across her jeans and struggled with a moment of confusion on how to greet Nathan—a hug, a kiss? He solved her dilemma when he reached her, placing a hand on her waist and drawing her to him. Her hands came up to rest on his chest, and he brushed a kiss on her cheek. "Lindsey," he greeted her in a husky murmur against her ear that sent a pleasant shiver down her spine.

"Nathan," Lindsey breathed as they parted to stand almost nose to nose. Gazing into his eyes, the world fell away, and Lindsey lost herself in the giddy joy of having him near, his chest warm and solid under her palm.

"Ahem. Hello? Earth to Lindsey." Makayla's voice intruded. "Are you going to introduce us?"

Breaking Nathan's gaze and stepping out of his embrace, Lindsey self-consciously turned to the table. "Nathan, this is Makayla." Lindsey gestured to her friend, who bounced in her seat as she extended her hand to Nathan.

He took it with a smile. "A pleasure to meet you."

"Likewise." Makayla beamed, all bubbly enthusiasm.

"And this is Charles. He sings in Jason's band."

Charles gave Lindsey a wounded look. "Since when is it Jason's band?" He sat forward from where he slumped in his chair and stretched to take Nathan's hand in a firm grip, before sinking back without another word. His pensive gaze remained on Nathan as he and Lindsey settled into their chairs.

"So, how did you meet?" Makayla asked, smiling at the couple, her eyes moving between them expectantly.

Lindsey hesitated. She should have known this was coming. She cast a questioning glance at Nathan. He gave her a warm smile and took her hand in his.

"Lindsey and I literally ran into each other a few years ago." Nathan turned toward Makayla. "I moved away and we lost touch until recently."

"Okaay," Makayla said. "So how did you two reconnect? Come on, guys, details."

Lindsey tightened her hold on Nathan and struggled to form a simple, uncomplicated answer that Makayla would accept and that she and Nathan could easily remember if asked again.

"Someone ordered rings?" a voice asked,

and the table turned their attention to the young woman who had spoken. She stood with her hip thrust to the side, holding out a basket heaped with onion rings and looking like she would rather be anywhere else.

"Those are mine." Makayla took the proffered basket.

The woman pivoted to leave, but then she straightened and offered a sultry, "Well, hey there." She twirled a piece of hair around her finger.

"Hey," came a deep, flat reply as Florian, the band's guitarist, approached the table. He stepped around the waitress without a second glance, and Lindsey heard Makayla snicker as the woman stalked away in a huff. "Makayla. Lindsey."

"Florian," Lindsey said. "I like the hair. The blue suits you much better."

Florian's mouth quirked into a lopsided grin as he pulled at his long bangs. "Yeah, the red was a bit much." He lowered his hand and looked at Nathan questioningly.

"I'm sorry," Lindsey said. "This is Nathan. Nathan, Florian."

The men exchanged a handshake.

"So what are you guys playing?" Nathan asked.

"A bit of this. Bit of that," Florian said. He clapped a hand on Charles's shoulder. "Come on. We're ready to play, and if we don't start soon, we're going to be tripping over the next group."

"All right." Charles got to his feet. "Ladies and gentleman, I take my leave." He offered them a salute, causing Florian to roll his eyes, and the two of them headed for the stage.

CHAPTER SEVENTEEN

MAKAYLA'S QUESTIONS PRIOR to the band taking the stage had been amiable and understandable, even if they had required some carefully thought-out replies. Throughout her gentle grilling, however, Nathan had been aware of Charles sitting there with his short, spiky white hair. The light fell across Charles's glasses in a way that obstructed a clear view of his eyes, but Nathan felt the man's silent scrutiny and believed that he was being weighed, measured, and in all likelihood found wanting. The occasional dark look Jason threw his way aggravated the sensation. The band's guitarist, Florian, had seemed indifferent to Nathan's presence, peering at him with only the barest hint of curiosity through long, blue-streaked bangs. Nathan doubted that neutrality would last. It had been a relief when the stage lights had come up and the rest of the room plunged into near darkness, effectively hiding Nathan from the band and stemming Makayla's questions as the music started.

Under other circumstances, Nathan suspected he would have enjoyed the evening. Jason's band, Suicidal Squirrels, played well, covering an eclectic mix of old and contemporary music. But Nathan dreaded what awaited him at the end of their set, and apprehension kept him from fully appreciating their efforts.

The band was now twenty minutes into their set. Lindsey had told him they would play for a half hour, which meant Nathan's reprieve had nearly reached its end. At best, he would have a few minutes of relative quiet to talk with Lindsey before the band joined them at the table. It was hardly enough time with her, and this was hardly the place to discuss dreamstriding, never mind trying to convince her to try consciously slipping into the dream realm with him. He wanted nothing more than to leave and wondered if Lindsey would be willing to go.

When the band finished their last song, the crowd erupted in applause and whistles. As the lights came back up and the noise died down, Nathan turned to Lindsey. Before he could make the suggestion to leave, Makayla grabbed his arm, her nails biting into his wrist and causing him to wince. She turned to him with enthusiasm. "Weren't they great?"

"Yes," Nathan agreed as he subtly tried to extricate himself from her grip. She continued to gaze at him with an air of expectancy, and Nathan offered the first thing that came to mind. "Jason plays really well."

Makayla released him, her hand moving to her chest. "Oh, I know. Doesn't he, though?" She gazed at the stage where the band talked to those who stood nearby. Flashing a quick grin at Nathan and Lindsey, she got to her feet. "All right, I'm going up there. Back in a bit." With a little wave she left them.

Nathan watched the petite brunette plow her way through the crowd. "She's a force to be reckoned with, isn't she?"

"Yes," Lindsey agreed with a fond smile.

"She likes Jason." He looked to Lindsey for confirmation.

"That's putting it mildly. Makayla and I were roommates our freshman year. I introduced them. She's been after him ever since."

He returned his attention to Makayla as she reached Jason's side, earning black looks from several women. In the face of Makayla's determination, Nathan almost felt a twinge of sympathy for Jason. Almost. She trailed after Jason as he coiled various cords. He paused once to shoot a dark look in Nathan's direction, and Nathan silently wished Makayla luck in capturing Jason's interest.

Leaning close to Lindsey, Nathan asked, "Do you want to get out of here? Or do we need to stay?"

"We can leave." She gave him a speculative look. "Did you have something in mind?"

"Are you hungry?"

"I could eat."

"Want to grab a late dinner? Or we could skip dinner and do dessert. Or you could come back to my place and…"

"Do dessert?" Her eyes sparkled with humor.

He smiled and ran the back of his knuckles lightly across her cheek, careful to avoid the fading bruise. "I was going to say try dream-striding."

The laughter faded from her eyes, and she pulled back slightly. Her brow furrowed. "Why?"

Nathan took her hand, but her fingers did not curl around his; they sat cool and unresponsive within his grasp. "Practice. To work on control."

Lindsey slowly shook her head. "Nathan—"

"I know I'm asking you to do something you don't really want to," he interrupted, "but Lindsey, as long as...Given the circumstances, you need more control."

She bit her lip and looked away. "Why dreamstride at all? Why not just stop?" She spoke so softly he could barely hear her.

"Lindsey." He waited for her to face him. "You may have retreated to your mountaintop, but you were still dreamstriding." He offered her an apologetic smile. "I found you, didn't I?"

Lindsey pulled her hand from his.

"If you can learn to consciously dreamstride, you can also consciously *not* dreamstride. If we go in together, then we can work together to improve both our skills. Who knows, you may be able to teach me how to teleport. Or shape-shift." He kept his tone conciliatory and hoped she would put aside her reluctance, but the longer she remained silent, biting her lip, looking anywhere but at him, the more certain he was that he had pushed too hard.

When she finally looked at him, he could see uncertainty in her eyes. She said, "Why don't we stop for takeout on the way to your place then take it from there?"

"Okay," Nathan said with a sense of relief.

"Do you want to stay here for a little longer, or should I go settle the tab?"

Lindsey looked to the stage, and Nathan did likewise. Jason stood glaring in their direction. "Why don't you go settle the tab."

Nathan leaned against the bar as the bartender grabbed a glass from the shelf above the registers and sorted through the small collection of credit cards. He withdrew one and checked the name against Nathan's license then rang up the tab. Nathan tapped his fingers and shot glances back to where he had left Lindsey.

"Here you go," the bartender said, sliding Nathan's card and a receipt toward him. Nathan added a tip and scrawled his signature across the bottom. Tucking his copy and his card into his wallet, he wended his way back to Lindsey and her friends.

As he got closer, he saw that Lindsey and Jason were having a heated exchange, based on her flushed face and stiff posture. Jason's voice, although indistinct, reached Nathan over the music being piped through the sound system.

"This is entirely different, and you know it." Lindsey's terse reply carried over to him. She caught his eye around Jason's shoulder, and Nathan thought he caught a flicker of relief mingled with the anger and hurt. She snatched her purse from the table and turned to Makayla. "I'm sorry. See you Monday?"

Makayla nodded, and Lindsey pushed past Jason.

"Lindsey," he barked as he turned to follow her. He grabbed her left arm and yanked her to a stop.

Nathan watched the color drain from Lindsey's face and felt sick at the obvious pain etched across her features. Without conscious thought, he crossed the space between them in two strides and ensnared Jason's wrist in a manacle-like grip. "Let her go."

Jason glared at him. "You stay out of this. This is between me and Lindsey."

"I don't think so." With no more than a handsbreadth between them, Nathan matched Jason's hostile gaze and spoke in low, biting tones. "Has it occurred to you that Lindsey may have injuries that you haven't seen?"

Jason's lips compressed into a tight line and his eyes narrowed. "But I suppose you've seen them."

Nathan's gaze remained unflinching. He felt the muscles in Jason's arm flex under his hand, heard Lindsey's breath hitch, and then Charles was there—insinuating himself between the two men, placing a hand on Jason's shoulder, his voice low and authoritative. "Jason, let go of Lindsey." When Jason failed to respond, Charles added, "You're hurting her."

Jason's eyes flicked to Charles, then past him to Lindsey. His hold on her loosened, she pulled away from him, and Nathan released Jason.

"I'll meet you upstairs," Lindsey threw over her shoulder then headed for the exit with Makayla close behind. Nathan leveled a glare at Jason. Stepping away from them, Charles muttered something incomprehensible and followed the women.

Nathan retrieved his coat from where it hung on the back of his chair. As he slid it on, he went to stand next to Jason. The muscles in his jaw worked as he stared ahead, trying to rein in his temper before speaking. "That's the second time you've manhandled her in my presence." He pinned Jason with a fierce look. "If it happens again, you and I are going to have it out."

They regarded each other with mutual animosity. Nathan started to walk away. "So tell me, dream-boy." Jason's soft drawl stopped him. "What do you want from her?"

"Nothing." Nathan spoke over his shoulder. "Just her."

"I don't think so." In his peripheral vision, Nathan saw Jason shaking his head as he came to stand shoulder to shoulder with him. "You want something from her, and she's going to be hurt when she finds out." Jason turned to face Nathan, but he continued looking straight ahead. "Hell, you're going to devastate her."

"And you'll be there. Waiting," Nathan sneered, turning to look at him. To his surprise, Jason looked mournful.

"Yeah, I will. Just like always." He turned away. Grabbing a beer off the table, he collapsed into a chair.

Nathan stalked through the crowd, exited the bar, and with salt crunching underfoot climbed the stairs to the street level. He found Lindsey there, huddled with Makayla under a small umbrella. Charles stood nearby, seemingly unconcerned with the snow that fell on him, making him look like some sort of bespectacled Unseelie prince. All three looked to Nathan as he cleared the top of the stairs. Makayla gave Lindsey's hand a squeeze then went to Charles's side.

Nathan stood in front of Lindsey.

"I forgot my gloves," she said, sounding small and lost.

He reached out and brushed her wet cheeks.

Placing his hand on the back of her neck, he gently drew her to him and folded her in his arms.

She buried her face against his chest. "I'm sorry."

He shook his head. "You have nothing to be sorry for."

She slid her arms under his jacket. Nathan bit his lip and tried not to flinch as the cold from her icy fingers penetrated his shirt. He rested his cheek on top of her head and breathed in the fruit-and-spice scent of her hair.

"Can we get out of here?" she asked.

"Of course. Are you still up for takeout and going to my place? Or would you like me to take you home?" he said, all thoughts of dreamstriding pushed to the background in the face of her distress.

"I don't want to go home." She lifted her chin and met his eyes. Nathan ran his knuckles along her jaw, lowered his head, and pressed a soft kiss to her lips. She leaned into him, and Nathan felt her hands curl into the fabric of his shirt. Feeling a bit dazed, he drew back and felt some satisfaction to see that she seemed a touch dazed herself.

Tucking her against his side, he went to lead her across the parking lot but found Makayla and Charles still there. Makayla bobbed from foot to foot trying to keep warm, worry written plainly on her face. Charles had his phone in hand, his thumb flying across it as he composed a text message.

"Makayla." Nathan offered his hand. "It was nice to meet you. I hope I'll see you again soon."

She placed her mitten-covered hand in his. "It was nice to meet you too."

Nathan turned to Charles, whose attention was firmly fixed on his phone. Charles frowned. His shoulders rose and fell with a sigh. "Right," he said, slipping the phone into a pocket. He looked at Lindsey and softly spoke her name, a hint of question in his voice.

She gave him a tremulous smile. "I'll be fine. Thank you, Charles."

He nodded to her and glanced at Nathan before turning to Makayla. "Come on, I'll give you a ride home."

She gave him a startled look. "But—"

Charles shook his head as he walked away. "You don't want to go back in." He paused when she failed to follow him. Looking back, he offered her reassurance. "Florian will get Jason home." He hooked his arm, offering it to her. With a parting look at Nathan and Lindsey, she accepted it, and the pair left.

Nathan felt the tension in Lindsey's frame. He gazed down at her troubled features, her bottom lip caught between her teeth. He wondered if they should call it a night, if he should take her home despite her willingness to continue with their plans. It would be the gentlemanly thing to do, but it felt right with her nestled against his side, and he wanted her with him.

"Do you like Chinese?" he asked.

Lindsey gave him a puzzled look. "I'm sorry?"

"Chinese. There's a place near where I live. It's close enough that the food would still be hot when we got it home."

"Sounds good."

He guided her across the parking lot, navigating around icy puddles. When they reached his car, he opened the door for her. Before she got in, he stroked a damp tendril from her cheek. "It's going to be okay, Lindsey. It'll all work out somehow." He took her hand and kissed her chilled fingers. "I promise."

CHAPTER EIGHTEEN

THE LIGHT SNOW-SHOWER turned into freezing rain, and forty-five minutes later, after being doused in the icy downpour on the brief walk from the car to the house, Lindsey stepped out of Nathan's bathroom dressed in the clothes he had lent her. His T-shirt fell nearly to her knees, and the sweat pants covered her feet almost as effectively as the thick wool socks. With her wet jeans and damp blouse in hand, she padded down the hall to the kitchen, where Nathan unpacked the takeout. He looked up as she entered.

"Better?" he asked, his voice lower than normal.

"Yes. Thank you." She held her clothes in front of her. "Where's your dryer?"

Nathan put a couple of plates on the counter then walked over and took her things. "I'll take care of them for you. Make yourself a plate. I'm going to change too—I'll be right back."

She watched him walk back the way she had come and heard him go up the stairs. The rich smell of the food fueled her appetite. She took a plate and loaded it with sticky rice and healthy portions of sweet-and-sour pork and General Tso's chicken. Making herself at home, she rummaged through the cabinets until she found a glass. She turned to fill it and found Nathan watching her, leaning against the doorframe.

Soundlessly, he walked with bare feet across the wood floor. His T-shirt pulled as he moved, hinting at the musculature underneath. Stopping in front of her, he tucked a piece of her hair behind her ear then slid his hand to the side of her neck. His thumb caressed her jaw. "I like seeing you here. In my home."

She raised her free hand to cover his, and they came together for a soft, lingering kiss. Lindsey curled her fingers around his wrist and felt his pulse beating a rapid rhythm to match the one he surely felt in her neck. They separated, but their gazes remained tangled.

"We should probably eat while the food is still hot," Nathan said.

Lindsey nodded. "Probably."

Nathan lowered his hand but captured Lindsey's in a gentle squeeze before stepping away to make his plate. "Dinner on the couch all right? Or would you prefer to sit here at the bar?"

"The couch is fine." She smiled. "It'll be like being at home."

"Then go ahead and get comfortable, and I'll be right there."

After filling her glass with water, Lindsey took her plate to the living room. Folding a leg underneath her, she sank onto the brown leather sofa. Nathan soon joined her. "Have you been able to catch up on your classes?"

"Most of them." Lindsey scooped some rice onto her fork. "My lit professor gave me an extension on my paper."

"That's good."

"Yes. She also gave me the number for a hotline for abused women." She took a bite.

Nathan winced. "Your friends think the same thing, don't they? That I hit you."

Lindsey nodded. "I've told them you didn't, but I also haven't given them another explanation, so I'm not sure they believe me."

"And Jason probably thinks I might as well be the one who hurt you, and holds me responsible." Nathan took a drink of his soda.

Lindsey looked down at her plate and

stabbed a water chestnut. "I don't think Jason believes the dream stuff." With a wry smile, she returned her attention to Nathan. "Sometimes I don't want to believe it either."

With a troubled expression clouding his features, Nathan reached out and laid a hand on Lindsey's knee. "Lindsey..."

"I saw on your business card that you work at the museum. Director of children's programming?"

Nathan withdrew his hand. "Yes, I coordinate and handle the installation of exhibits from area schools. I also develop summer programs, and more recently programs to take into schools that have had their art programs closed down because of budget cuts."

"Very cool. It sounds like a fun and rewarding job."
"Most of the time."

"And is that your studio in the front room?" Lindsey asked.

"Yes, it is."

"Do I get to see some of your paintings while I'm here?"

"If you'd like. I'd be happy to show them to you, although some of the better ones are at the gallery." He picked up his egg roll and dragged it through a small puddle of sauce. "One of my favorites, however, is here." He smiled at Lindsey. "It's a painting of you."

"Of me?" Lindsey lowered her fork.

"Yep."

"But, when? How?"

"A few years ago. From memories of you in dreams." He grinned then continued with pride, "I've had more than one offer for it." His voice softened. "But I haven't been able to part with it. Any time I've shown it, I've half hoped, expected, that someone would walk in and recognize you. Tell me where to find you." He lowered his eyes, looking abashed.

Lindsey felt a knot form in her chest. Despite everything, he had still been looking for her. "I want to see it."

"Of course."

She scraped her fork against the plate, gathering the remaining rice and pork into a neat pile. "Nathan? How did you find me?"

He put his empty plate on the coffee table and faced Lindsey. "It's one of those things that I can tell you what happened, but I can't explain why it worked."

"Okay."

"When you got shot, when you left the dream, you left part of yourself behind. At least that's the best way I can describe it. There was blood and feathers. One of the feathers—I picked it up, and I could *feel* you."

Lindsey felt a chill run up her spine and her mouth went dry.

"From it, I got all these images and feelings. I used the images to help me find you. It took a couple of days to make sense of them." Nathan laughed without humor, and his eyes revealed his own unease. "I'm not a big fan of the idea of fate or destiny, so I'm going to credit luck with you being nearby—in a city I know fairly well. That the university is a big part of your life right now helped too."

Lindsey put aside her plate. "Could you have found me before this?"

"No, I don't see how I could have. Not without asking you directly in a dream."

Lindsey drew her knees up and wrapped her arms around them. "Which you could have done. Whenever you wanted."

"Yes," he said with a look of consternation. "Lindsey, I am truly sorry. If I could go back and—"

She waved aside his words. "I'm not looking for another apology, Nathan. I'm just trying to understand how we got here." Her foot bobbed up and down on the leather upholstery. "Don't get me wrong. What you did was awful, and I get pissed when I start thinking about it. I mean, really, of all the asinine..." Taking a deep breath, she unfolded her legs and let them slide down to her side, but the tension remained in her body and between her and Nathan—thick, heavy, and silent enough to hear the hum of the dryer down the hall.

She met Nathan's gaze. His look of worry and concern turned penitent as he slid close. He wrapped a curl around his finger before tucking it behind her ear. "Can you forgive me? Will we be able to get past it?"

"I think so. I want to. But, Nathan." She took hold of his hand. "Don't ever lie to me again. Not even to protect me."

He lowered his eyes to their clasped hands. "I won't." He grazed the back of her hand with his lips then turned his brilliant blue eyes to her. She drew her bottom lip between her teeth.

He leaned closer. "Every time you do that"—his voice deepened and grew husky—"I want to do this." His hands framed her face as he covered her mouth with his and sucked her lip between his teeth before releasing it to kiss her.

Lindsey wrapped her arms around his neck and held him close. When he eased her under him and she felt his hands slide under her shirt, skim up her sides, and settle against her just under her breasts, only one thought filled her mind: *Finally.*

Finally, despite thinking him lost, despite what he had done, she had him back. She could touch him, taste him, and fulfill all the longing and attraction that simmered between them in the dreams and here in this moment. Finally, the half-formed yearnings and longings that she had just begun to understand when he disappeared could be fulfilled. Finally, she had Nathan.

She moaned in protest when he pulled back. He rested his forehead against hers. "Not here," he said around ragged breaths. "I really like this couch, Lindsey, but I don't want this to be where I make love with you for the first time." He kissed her and got to his feet.

Lindsey accepted the hand he offered and allowed him to draw her up after him. He caressed her cheek and pulled her close. She pressed her lips against the side of his neck then trailed kisses up until she reached his ear. "I would offer to race you to the bedroom." She nipped his earlobe, eliciting a groan from him. "But I'm not sure where it is."

"Just follow me," he said, and led her toward the stairs. They stopped more than once before reaching his bedroom, their pauses both playful and urgent. Halfway up the stairs, Nathan's shirt came off at Lindsey's insistent urging. She took a moment to enjoy the sight before running her hands over his chest and setting her lips over his heart. He entangled his fingers in her hair, pulled her mouth to his, and kissed her with enough force to leave her lips feeling swollen. Gathering her in his arms, he carried her up the last couple of steps and into the bedroom.

After setting her next to the bed, Nathan gazed at her for a moment. "You're beautiful. I don't think I've ever told you that. Every time I look at you, it hits me all over again just how beautiful you are." Lindsey's vision started to blur with tears. Nathan put his arms around her and buried his face against her neck. "And you smell so good."

Lindsey felt his hands move down her back to her hips. Her breath quickened in anticipation as he gathered the fabric of her shirt and eased it upward. He stepped back, and she raised her arms so he could draw the shirt over her head. His eyes fell to the bruises that still marred her skin. He ran his fingers over the one below her sternum. His touch was light and barely felt, but she shivered under it. "How bad is it?" He looked at her with concern. "I don't want to hurt you."

"That one and the one on my back don't bother me anymore."

"So, this," he said as he bent low, his mouth hovering near her navel, his hands firmly on her hips, "won't be a problem?" He touched his tongue to her sensitive skin and trailed it up until he reached the lace of her bra, looking at her through thick lashes that only men seemed to come by naturally.

"Not a problem," she said, feeling weak in the knees.

"Good." He nearly purred, sounding pleased with himself. He slid a hand to the small of her back as he straightened. With his other hand, he ran the back of his fingers along her left arm, wrist to shoulder, leaving goose bumps in their wake. Lindsey felt him tense as he looked at her shoulder. "I don't need to ask about this."

"It won't be a problem." Lindsey skimmed a finger down his side. "Not for you."

"No?" he asked and flinched when she found a ticklish spot.

"No." She shook her head and stepped into him until the length of their bodies were flush and she had to tip her chin to meet his gaze. "Being an artist, you must be creative." With her hands on his shoulders to balance herself, Lindsey rose up on her toes and enjoyed the feel of skin moving against skin. She kissed his jaw, and his breathing quickened. "Imaginative." She nipped his neck, and his hand moved up to the middle of her back, his fingers tense against her spine. A small, feminine smile curved her lips at his response. "Inventive." She kissed the corner of his mouth, and before she could withdraw, he changed the angle of the kiss, crushing her to him, leaving them both breathing hard.

"That almost sounded like a challenge, Lindsey."

"And if it was?" Her breath caught on the last word at the feel of her bra loosening. Watching her with passion-darkened eyes, he carefully lifted the left shoulder strap so that no part of it dragged against the bruises.

"I happily accept."

Lindsey lay curled on her side snuggled against Nathan. Her head rested on his shoulder. His heart beat a solid, steady rhythm under her hand. Her eyes fell closed at the pleasant sensation of Nathan playing with her hair, gentle little pulls as he raked his fingers through it. With a contented sigh, she burrowed closer to him. "That feels nice. You could put me to sleep doing that." She stifled a yawn.

"Sleep if you're tired, Linds."

She stretched her arm across his chest and listened to him breathe. "I'm not a real fan of sleep right now." Nathan's hand stilled in her hair. "I've been going as long as I can without it."

"Because of the dreamstriding."

"Yes."

"That's not healthy." Nathan embraced her then resumed toying with her hair. When he spoke again, the words came slowly. "Will you let me teach you how to dreamstride on purpose? It might help."

Lindsey's stomach knotted at the idea. She chewed on her lip. "Might?"

"I can dreamstride pretty much whenever I want, but I do still find myself doing it without meaning to."

Lindsey traced idle patterns across his chest. "Then what's the point? I don't want to do it, Nathan." Her brow furrowed at how petulant she sounded, but she added, "I already end up there more than I want."

Nathan captured her hand. "Because, I recognize it as soon as a dream shifts into dreamstriding and can get out of there. I want you to be able to do the same thing." He kissed her fingertips. "I'm trying to keep you safe."

Lindsey withdrew her hand and propped

herself up so she could see his face. "This is important to you."

He cupped her cheek. "You're important to me."

"What do I do?"

"Relax," he said as she settled next to him again. His voice rumbled under her ear. "Let yourself go to sleep, but be aware of what's happening. The way you lose sense of where your arms and legs are. The way your whole body drops away and leaves just you. Think about where you want to be when you dream-stride, then ride that thought there."

"Do you have any idea how hokey that sounds?" Lindsey grumbled.

"Yes." He sighed. "Trust me. Try it."

"Fine." She closed her eyes and tried to think of where she wanted to be if what Nathan told her worked. She rejected her hill; it no longer felt safe. Nathan's diner was likewise not a good choice. She thought to ask Nathan for a suggestion or some guidance but realized that his hand, which had been playing with her hair, had stilled, and his breathing had fallen into slow, even breaths.

Without a clear destination in mind, based on what Nathan had said she would not be walking the dream realm tonight, not intentionally at least. The relief that Lindsey felt at that realization spread throughout her body and allowed her to truly relax. It also forced her to recognize how she was pushing herself to do something just to please Nathan. In the morning she would have to talk to him about it. Lindsey's awareness of her body fell away. She roused briefly, remembering there had been something else she needed to talk about with Nathan, something Lawrence had said when they had been in his garden. The image of a small bridge crossing a stream in a Japanese garden flickered through her thoughts as sleep claimed her.

CHAPTER NINETEEN

IT TOOK A moment for Lindsey to orient herself as colors and forms shifted in a psychedelic mash that left her feeling like she had fallen into the fabric of a tie-dye T-shirt. As the colors muted and solidified, she turned in a slow circle, assessing her surroundings. Recognizing the landscape and the teahouse, Lindsey groaned and hung her head. She recalled her final thoughts and the image that had come to mind as she had fallen asleep. Apparently, Nathan's method worked. She peered at the teahouse with a sense of self-disgust. For all of their talk about how to dreamstride, not once had she asked nor had Nathan explained how to get out. The only method that she knew involved violence and pain. Lindsey scowled. If Lawrence was around, he might be happy to oblige her.

Casting her senses wide, Lindsey searched

for Nathan or Lawrence and his group. Disappointment vied with relief when she failed to detect any sign of another dreamstrider. Now what? How was she supposed to find Nathan? Should she wait for him, or start walking and hope that they would find each other?

Screwing her eyes shut tight, Lindsey tipped her head back and bit her lip until she tasted a coppery tang. "Damn." She raised her hand to her mouth. Looking at the blood that stained her fingertips, her shoulders slumped. "This is stupid."

Dejected, she made her way to the teahouse and settled herself on one of the smooth wooden steps. A hollow clunk sounded at regular intervals, mingling with the soothing murmur of the stream. She closed her eyes and considered the possibility of truly falling asleep and exiting the dream realm that way. That had worked before, hadn't it?

The hollow *clunk* resounded, sending a tremor through the garden. Lindsey's eyes flew open and her breath caught. She began to scour the garden for any visible differences.

A faint noise came from behind her. A thin line of golden light appeared to her left, falling across the steps to the ground. The barest hint of another's presence brushed against her awareness. Accompanied by a soft whoosh, the light expanded until it spilled over her, casting her huddled shadow before her. While the light felt warm and welcoming, she perceived the presence that grew apace with it—that encroached upon her senses—as cool and stinging. Climbing to her feet, Lindsey gathered herself and, with chin raised and shoulders braced, turned to confront the man behind her. "Lawrence."

He stood in the entrance to the teahouse, his hand still resting on the edge of the shoji screen, his expression stern. The pair spent a moment sizing each other up. Lawrence stepped to the side. "Close the door behind you," he said as he retreated inside.

Lindsey hesitated. Having expected more opprobrious comments, his abrupt invitation surprised her. Recognizing, however, that he could provide her with much-needed answers, she stifled her trepidation and followed him, pausing in the doorway to carefully slide the screen closed until it abutted the frame and formed a tight, seamless seal. She warily faced Lawrence.

He sat at a kotatsu. In front of him rested a small teapot decorated in a delicate cherry blossom motif. He lifted a matching cup and inhaled the rising steam. In contrast to the tension Lindsey felt, he seemed surprisingly serene. He looked at her over the rim of his cup. "Sit."

Lindsey lowered herself next to the low table and slid her legs underneath the heavy blanket that skirted it. Lawrence continued to regard her. Unlike the last time she had seen him, nothing of what he felt leaked from him. She fidgeted under his gaze, feeling like she had been called to the principal's office. Once more he inhaled the steam before taking a sip. The action caught Lindsey's attention and she looked at him in puzzlement. "Why?"

"That's a rather broad question," he said, lowering the cup and gazing into it. "Perhaps you would care to be more precise?"

Lindsey ground her teeth. "Why do you inhale the steam when there are no scents here?"

"You assume that what you experience here holds true for everyone." He drank again.

"You can smell it?"

"No." Lawrence smirked. Dark amusement shone in his eyes. "But the ritual soothes me."

Lindsey dug her nails into her palms, dropped her chin, and closed her eyes, trying to contain her irritation. Taking a deep breath, she looked at Lawrence and met his critical gaze. "Why do you hate me?"

"I do not hate you. I simply do not respect you."

Remembering the scene in the garden, Lindsey snorted. "Oh, it goes beyond disrespect."

Lawrence scowled and looked into his teacup. He rotated it within his grasp. "Perhaps it does."

"Why?"

Lawrence carefully set his cup on the surface of the kotatsu. He loosely folded his hands and rested them on the edge of the table. "You're wild." His hard gaze met hers. "Out of control. Dangerous. You put everyone around you at risk." The light in the teahouse dimmed. Lawrence closed his eyes and flattened his palms on the kotatsu. He took a deep breath and held it for a few heartbeats before slowly releasing it. The teahouse brightened. Without looking at Lindsey, he continued, "You warp the fabric around you." He picked up his tea. "In that respect, you and Nathan's killer—the young man who pursues you—are alike."

Frozen by outrage and a sickening fear that Lawrence might be right, that he might possess knowledge of her actions in previous dreams that she had long forgotten, Lindsey watched him as he drank his tea. When he glanced at her she stammered, "I—I never—"

"No." His expression thawed but remained studied.

Relief surged through Lindsey.

"But, like him, you are capable of giving things more heft."

Lindsey recalled the changes Nathan had noted in the dream realm, how things had taken on more..."Substance."

"Exactly."

"You said I had no skill."

"And you don't." A superior glint shone in his eyes. "Raw power, yes. But skill? No."

"Semantics." Lindsey glared at him.

"A crucial distinction."

"Are you a politician out there in the real world?" Lindsey asked in exasperation, and to her surprise Lawrence laughed, a deep guffaw that echoed with warmth and mirth and temporarily brightened the teahouse like the noonday sun.

"No." Genuine humor lit his face. "I have no patience for fools." His shoulders still shaking with laughter, Lawrence held out his hand so that it hovered over the kotatsu, and a teacup appeared under it. He carefully poured tea into it then pushed it across to Lindsey.

Warily, she watched him and took the cup. The pleasing warmth that penetrated the sides of the thin porcelain startled her. Without thinking she raised it and breathed in the steam. When she realized that she had unwittingly mimicked Lawrence despite knowing there would be no aroma, she winced and waited for him to mock her, but when she glanced at him over the rim of the cup, he merely smiled, a slight quirk at the corner of his mouth that was almost gone before she could register it.

"Why did you come here, Lindsey?"

"I didn't mean to." Lawrence tilted his head and waited. Lindsey traced a finger over the cherry blossom pattern on the cup. "Nathan was trying to teach me how to get here. Well, not *here* here, but to dreamstride, and I ended up here."

A pained look crossed Lawrence's face. "He goes to you for help and ends up teaching you."

Lindsey looked down, her hands tightened around the cup, and she bit her lip. "This isn't the first time you've said something about him coming to me for help."

"No." Lawrence's response was both question and statement. Unable to ask for a further explanation, fearful of the answer, Lindsey silently pleaded with Lawrence. Pity touched his eyes. "What reason has Nathan given you for breaking his self-imposed exile and suddenly reappearing in your life?"

She swallowed and put the cup on the kotatsu; it rattled against the wood surface. "To warn me. To protect me." Lawrence's features pinched as he glanced away from her, seemingly reluctant to meet her eyes. "Did he lie?"

"This is a conversation you need to have with Nathan."

"Lawrence." Anguish filled Lindsey's voice.

With a heavy sigh of resignation, Lawrence said, "You were perfectly safe. No one could have reached you if you hadn't permitted it."

"Not even Nathan?"

"Not even him."

Lindsey focused on the teacup within her hands, wishing that its warmth could chase away the chill she felt building inside her. "Then he did lie."

"By omission and, perhaps, ignorance." Lindsey looked up in confusion, and Lawrence continued, "Nathan's not as knowledgeable of this place as he would like to believe. His desire to protect you—his desire *for* you—is genuine. However, that is not his sole motivation, and he failed to understand how well insulated you were. The only door left open was the one for him, and I suspect that was an unconscious doing on your part. Why shield yourself from someone you had trusted and believed dead?" Lindsey lowered her gaze, shied away from the compassion in Lawrence's eyes. "It would be best if you stopped coming here."

Lindsey shook her head. "It's not like I plan to be here." Anger and frustration welled up inside her and colored her words. "I don't want to be here."

"Then you need to construct a new place for yourself and keep everyone out, including Nathan," he said, his voice stern and uncompromising.

"You say it like it's so easy, but I don't know where to start."

"With the spheres."

"What spheres?" Lindsey's voice rose in volume.

With a familiar look of disdain, Lawrence held out his hand and snapped his fingers. A small gold sphere like the one in the garden appeared above the table, hovering like a newborn star.

"That? Your little ball of light?"

"Yes."

"That's your solution?"

"Yes," Lawrence snapped. A muscle jumped along the side of his face, and the light wavered in the teahouse. "You've always been so difficult. So contrary."

"Stop judging me by who I was. I was little more than a child."

"You're *still* little more than a child."

Lindsey rolled her eyes and huffed a sigh.

"Listen. For once, listen and pay attention."

Lindsey crossed her arms in front of her and shot him a sullen glance.

"The sphere..." Lawrence cupped his hand under it and it settled on his fingertips. "...is a miniature of what you need to construct. Make one of these, expand it until it encompasses you, stay within it, and no one can reach you unless you permit it." His sharp eyes challenged her. "Where do you think you sit right now?"

Perplexed, Lindsey looked around the room.

"Do you truly not see it?" Lawrence rubbed at his forehead as if to ease a headache.

"Didn't you recently criticize me for assuming that what I experience here holds true for everyone?"

"Indeed." After waving away the sphere, he reached across the table. "Take my hand." Lindsey did as he instructed, letting her hand rest lightly against his, but he slid his hand further underneath hers until he grasped her around the wrist. "Now see as I do."

Lindsey's fingers closed reflexively around

Lawrence's wrist as the sense of being pulled under the ocean's tide swept over her. She gasped and coughed against the suffocating sensation, but then it receded and the world around her looked different, having no more substance than a projected image flickering against a blank void. Lawrence's voice echoed through her. "We make this place. It has only what we bring. There are no rules but those we impose. This is why we must be cautious."

Dazed, Lindsey pulled free from Lawrence. She stood and approached one of the walls. Behind it, through it, she saw a barrier of some sort. Somewhere between black and the darkest of silvers, it shimmered with the movement of a torrential rain hitting glass, only it moved in all directions with some semblance of a pattern. "This is how you see?"

"When I choose to look deeper, yes."

Lindsey tentatively placed her hand on the wall. Despite its transparency it felt solid. With a little shove, her hand passed through. She tried to touch the barrier, but it repelled her hand like an oppositely charged magnet. The shimmering shield absorbed her attention, and she jumped when Lawrence spoke at her shoulder. "Would you care to see it from the outside?"

From the corner of her eye, she saw him offer his hand. Bracing herself for another flood of sensation, she grasped his hand and felt a wave of vertigo as her perception slipped and turned before settling above where she stood. Below her was the sphere, its surface smooth and polished like a black pearl. It looked impenetrable. A quick glance revealed others glimmering across the horizon.

"This is what you must construct if you are to stay safe from the one who hunts you," Lawrence said. His words snapped Lindsey back to the teahouse. She removed her hand from his and studied him.

Lawrence had mentioned the other dreamstrider before. At the time Lindsey had been distracted, unsettled by being compared to her pursuer, and worried that she might have been a similar monster. "You told your group that he was a phantom. That there was no killer."

"Yes," Lawrence said, his expression closed.

Lindsey frowned. "But you know he's real. You know what he's done."

"Of course." He turned away and resumed his position by the kotatsu. With a careless wave of his hand the tea set disappeared.

Lindsey trailed after him and sank to her knees by the low table. "You're lying to them. Why?"

"They're in no danger," he said with calm certainty. "I see no point in frightening them."

Lindsey stared at him in bewilderment. How could he say that with such conviction? What assurance did he have that his group would escape slaughter? She leaned across the table and gazed into Lawrence's eyes, silently daring him to look away, and then she knew with the same certainty as if he had told her. "You've talked to him." Lawrence flinched and looked away. "You know who he is."

"No." Lawrence shook his head. "Not really."

"But you know something. Did you make a deal with him? Do you know why he's doing this?" When he remained silent and refused to meet her gaze, she slapped the table. "Dammit, Lawrence. What do you know?" Small fissures opened under her hand and crept across the table. Tendrils of blue energy jumped the gaps.

Lawrence looked at the kotatsu, his mouth twisted in irritation, and said, "Get control of yourself. I did not make a deal with him. There was no need once I made it clear that no one in the group can give him what he wants."

"And exactly what does he want?"

"He wants to die."

Lindsey frowned, and Lawrence ran a hand

over the table's surface, snuffing out the blue flames and sealing the cracks. "He is either incapable or unwilling to do the deed himself in the waking world. I'm not sure which. Quite honestly, I kept our contact as brief as possible. As for committing suicide here...Well, it's about as effective as trying to kill yourself by holding your breath." He sighed. "He asked for my help, but I refused. He threatened, and I still refused. At some point, Zach, Sarah, and Nathan caught his attention. None of them proved capable of giving the young man what he desires, although I do not doubt Nathan would if he could." Lawrence looked at her with troubled eyes. "And so, the young man continues his search for someone to assist him."

"Me."

"It seems so." Lawrence nodded.

Chills pricked along Lindsey's skin. Her chest felt tight. "Lawrence, every time I've encountered him, he's tried to kill me."

"He's testing you, most likely. Your strength and abilities. Are you a match for him? Can you give him what he wants?"

"I can't." Lindsey buried her face in her shaking hands. "I plan to apply to med school. Killing someone...I just can't."

"Even if it means saving your own life? Because I suspect his attacks are also an attempt to provoke you into performing the deed."

Lindsey looked at Lawrence in despair. "How did he even find me? That first time, he welcomed me back. He knew my *name*." She trembled in agitation. "Did you tell him about me?"

"No," he said, not quite maintaining eye contact. "But Nathan and I had more than one argument about his approaching you. I can't be certain that one of our altercations wasn't over-heard."

"And Nathan led him right to me." Lind-sey's stomach clenched.

"If you wish to avoid conflict..."

Lindsey heard Lawrence begin, but then her head spun and his voice sounded garbled and distant. She placed her hand on the table to steady herself. Her stomach knotted again, and acid burned the back of her throat. Her hand slipped across the smooth surface of the kotat-su, and she fell forward, cracking her forehead on the wood. Strong hands gripped her shoul-ders and pulled her upright. Her chin seemed determined to rest against her chest despite her efforts to raise it. She whimpered in relief when someone raised it for her. She blinked furiously, trying to pull her vision into focus. Lawrence's face swam before her, and her hearing cleared enough to hear him mutter, "Fool."

Light flared in the teahouse. The sudden burst left spots in her vision, but she considered them a small price to pay for the sudden cessation of her disorientation and pain.

Lawrence stood over her, scowling at the shoji screen. "Nathan is outside. The fool has tethered himself to you somehow. Wherever you go in this place, he'll be able to find you. Even here." Lawrence glared down at her. "You wouldn't know how he's managed that, would you?"

Lindsey glanced at the screen. "He can find me anywhere?"

"Here. Yes."

"Maybe not just here." She told him what Nathan had done with one of her feathers.

Lawrence folded his arms across his chest and his expression darkened. "Yes, I suppose that would do it. But only you..." He covered his eyes with his hand. "He found you out there, didn't he? In the real world?"

"Yes."

"Are you with him at this moment?"

Heat spread across Lindsey's cheeks and her eyes stung. "Yes."

"Am I correct that you would rather put off

seeing him for a bit longer?"

Lindsey closed her eyes and nodded.

"Then come on," he said in exasperation. "I can only imagine what effect a quarrel between the two of you would have here. I too would rather you postpone it."

Lindsey opened her eyes and found Lawrence watching her, his hand outstretched to help her stand. "But if he can find me anywhere…?"

"Finding and following are two different things, and there are some places he cannot go." Lindsey took Lawrence's hand and allowed him to pull her to her feet. A wicked light of amusement touched his eyes. "Do you think you're up to a little flying tonight?"

"Flying?" Lindsey recalled soaring through the air as a hawk. She glanced at the screen that hid her from Nathan then looked to Lawrence. "He can't?"

"No, he can't. At least not like you. He will be able to find you but unable to reach you." Lawrence's smile had a hard edge.

Lindsey looked at the screen once more and decided she wanted whatever time she could get to gather her thoughts, so that when she faced Nathan she would be prepared. "Yes."

"Very well, then. I will open the barrier, and

you take wing."

"Okay," she said, not at all certain she could do it.

Lawrence crossed to the opposite side of the teahouse. He placed a hand on the wall then looked at her. "Lindsey, I won't let you near them, the group, but if you ever want to hone your abilities..."

"Limit them, you mean."

He raised an eyebrow. "Do I seem limited to you?"

Yes hovered on the tip of her tongue, but she forced herself to objectively consider the question. "No."

"Just so." He ran his hand down the wall, ripping apart the fabric of the barrier. "Now, fly."

Focusing on her memories of flying, Lindsey took a handful of hurried steps toward the opening. She flapped her wings and soared into the night sky. She rode the currents high into the clouds and floated among them. She buried all sense of herself as Lindsey and submerged herself in the sensations of her new form. Once, she felt a strange, distant pull, as if the ground were calling out to her and begging her to land. Curious, she circled lower and surveyed the valley floor, but, seeing only a man and no prey, she ignored the impulse and returned to the heights until true sleep claimed her.

CHAPTER TWENTY

LINDSEY WOKE TO the weight of Nathan's hand settling on her hip. He brushed a kiss on her shoulder then got out of bed. A draft of cold air hit her back before the blankets cocooned her once more. She kept her eyes closed and feigned sleep as he shuffled through the room. She listened to the soft whoosh of drawers opening and closing, the click of the bathroom door shutting, and the gurgle-clank of old pipes as water flowed through them.

As soon as she heard the shower running, Lindsey flipped onto her back and hugged the blankets close to her. She stared at the ceiling, grey in the predawn light. Her chest felt tight and her heart beat an uncomfortable staccato. The thoughts that crowded her mind—memories of conversations with Nathan and with Lawrence—so overwhelmed her that they defied her ability to put them into words, leaving a numb void in their place.

Closing her eyes, she swallowed hard and tried to ignore an increasing sense of nausea. However brief it had been, Lawrence had given her the gift of time and space, but now she needed to face Nathan with what she knew and try to wrest the full truth from him. She pulled the covers over her head and stifled a small sob. Why did it have to be this way? She felt like a fool.

Angry with herself, she drew in a ragged breath and swiped the tears from her cheeks. Throwing back the blankets, she got out of bed, gasping as her feet hit the cold floor. She put on her undergarments and the shirt Nathan had lent her then went in search of the laundry room; if she was going to face him, she wanted to be dressed, not naked and in his bed.

After finding her clothes, Lindsey put herself together the best she could, rinsing her mouth, splashing water on her face, and finger-combing her hair. She heard the pipes go silent as the shower shut off. She cast an uneasy glance at the ceiling, picturing Nathan moving around above her as the floor creaked with his steps. Rejecting the idea of returning to his bedroom, Lindsey wandered into his studio.

The first painting to catch her attention sat on an easel near the window—a blend of red and black with deep purples and blue in sharp contrast to a thin series of white streaks edged in yellow. The streaks seemed to sweep downward and appeared to struggle out from under the thick, oppressive colors. The shapes and swirls that floated around the white evoked a sense of unease, and Lindsey hugged herself as she stepped closer. She narrowed her eyes as she studied it and the seemingly random flow of strokes resolved into a face. The portrait was a rough approximation, almost a caricature, but Lindsey recognized it. Her breath caught in her throat, and she retreated a step.

"Not my best work," Nathan said, making her jump. "But then, it was really more for catharsis." He walked into Lindsey's field of vision, obscuring her view of the painting. Using both hands, he picked up the canvas by the edges and added it to a pile against the wall. After a quick look at his hands, Nathan put them in the back pockets of his jeans. He turned to Lindsey. "If I had known you were up, I would have invited you to share the shower." His teasing tone sounded forced, and a wary glint shone in his eyes.

Lindsey bit her lip then blushed as she remembered what Nathan had said last night about this particular nervous gesture and what had followed. Fidgeting under his steady scrutiny, she broke eye contact and shuffled back a step, uncertain how to start the conversation that needed to happen.

"Second thoughts, Linds?" She froze at the pain and vulnerability that laced his voice. "Regrets?"

That single word, uttered so softly as to be almost inaudible, broke through Lindsey's internal barriers and stirred the chaos she had sought to submerge. She struggled as words of reassurance vied with questions and demands for answers. Hot tears spilled down her cheeks as she shook her head in denial. She looked around the studio, everywhere—anywhere—but directly at Nathan, and her eyes fell on another of his paintings. She recognized the subject of this painting, too; it was her. "That's the painting you were telling me about last night."

In her peripheral vision, Lindsey saw Nathan rake his fingers through his hair. "Yes."

She walked over to it, wiping at her tears as she went.

"What do you think?" There was an edge to his voice.

Lindsey considered the painting, trying to

be objective and ignore that she was the subject matter. "You're talented. You do beautiful work. I'm a bit envious. I can't manage much more than stick figures." Nathan made no reply, and Lindsey found the growing silence unsettling. She looked over her shoulder and met his shuttered gaze. "Have you always been able to see me in dreams? Clearly?"

Nathan appeared surprised by the question. "Most of the time."

She gestured to the painting. "Have you seen me like this?"

"Yes."

Lindsey pivoted to face him. "When?"

"I don't know. Before..." Nathan threw his hands in the air. "The painting isn't based on one specific dream."

"So you've seen me like this more than once."

"Yes." Nathan started to reach for her but then pulled back when she stiffened at the motion. "Lindsey, what's this about? Talk to me."

She squared her shoulders and forced herself to maintain eye contact, hoping his solemn blue eyes would not confirm her fear that her misgivings were well founded, that Lawrence was correct, that Nathan wanted more from her than he had yet to admit. Drawing a deep breath, she asked, "Why did you come find me on my hill?"

"I've already told you, Lindsey. To keep you safe. To warn you." His tone was guarded, bordering on patronizing.

"I talked with Lawrence last night."

Nathan's jaw tightened. "The teahouse. You were there."

"Yes."

"And?"

"Lawrence told me that I was already safe. According to him, you were likely the only person who could reach me before now. He suggested you had another reason."

Nathan scowled. "Really? And what might that be? Did he say? And since when are you friends with Lawrence? Since when do you trust him more than me?"

She studied Nathan through narrowed eyes. "Since you dodged the question. He's right, isn't he? You want my help." He turned away and walked to the window. "This has never been about keeping me safe, has it? Even in the beginning, when you brought me my sword, that wasn't about being able to protect myself, was it?"

Nathan shoved his hands into his front pockets and hunched his shoulders. He delivered a series of light kicks to the leg of the easel, and then he turned to Lindsey.

"It wasn't even about this," she went on, gesturing back and forth between them. "Was it?"

"That's not true." His steady voice cut through her rising panic. She started to feel a sense of relief, but it was cut short. "Not entirely. I've regretted cutting myself off from you. I've wondered how you are. Where you are. What might have been if I hadn't done what I did. Wondered if you would let me in again." He captured a piece of her hair and ran its length between his fingers. He tucked it behind her ear, and Lindsey steeled herself against her desire to lean into him and seek his embrace.

"But?"

Nathan lowered his hand. A cold distance took root in his gaze. "What Lawrence told you about me wanting your help was true."

"Help with what?"

"It doesn't matter anymore. I'm going to make coffee. You want some?" He stalked past her.

Stunned by his abrupt departure, Lindsey stood still, gaping in disbelief. "It doesn't matter?" Fury stirred at Nathan's dismissive attitude, and she started to tremble. "Right. Sure.

Okay." Ready for battle, she gritted her teeth and went to the kitchen, where she found Nathan refilling the water reservoir for the coffee maker. "The hell it doesn't matter!"

Nathan dropped the reservoir in the sink and water splashed up onto his shirt. He cast an irritated look at Lindsey. Lawrence had been wise to put off this confrontation, because at the sight of that look, at the thought that Nathan would dare to be angry with her in that moment, Lindsey wanted nothing more than to crush him, to grind him into a pulp until her sense of betrayal faded, and a small voice deep inside told her that in the dream realm she was fully capable of doing so.

When she spoke, her words came slow and measured. "You came to me in a place that no one else could find. You led a murderer to me. A murderer who now knows my name. Who seems intent on pursuing me until one of us is dead. I've been chased. I've been run through and shot. I spent a night vomiting and was bedridden for days because of those injuries. I hardly sleep anymore. All of this, thanks to you. And you don't think it matters. It matters."

Nathan leaned against the counter, reminding Lindsey of how he had stood waiting for her in her own kitchen not even a week ago. He worked a dish towel over his hands. "It doesn't matter." He tossed the towel onto the counter and walked over to her, close enough to make Lindsey uncomfortable, but she remained firm and refused to yield ground to him. "It hasn't mattered since I found you in your apartment. I didn't expect that, Lindsey. I didn't expect us. But once I found you, I knew that what I had wanted didn't matter anymore. You matter. Only you." He shook his head. "I'll figure out the rest on my own."

"It matters to me. You told me last night that you wouldn't lie to me, but you've lied from the beginning." She placed her hand over his heart. "Tell me, Nathan, or we don't have a chance."

Nathan closed his eyes. When he opened them again, he gazed over her shoulder. "I wanted you to help me kill the bastard."

Lindsey stepped back. Her hand remained suspended in the air at the level of his heart. The space between their bodies suddenly felt bitterly cold. "What?"

His eyes cut to hers. A hard, unforgiving light shone in them. "You heard me."

"But, Nathan...Kill him?"

"Yes."

Lindsey shook her head. "You can't. You wouldn't. It would be—"

"Wrong?" Nathan sneered. He moved forward, and Lindsey shuffled back. "If not that, then what?"

"I don't know."

"What do you propose we do?"

"I don't know." Lindsey turned her back on him and took a few hurried steps away until she found herself at the entrance to his studio. The dark portrait of the killer seemed to glare at her. She rubbed her hands up and down her arms, trying to ward off the cold inside.

Nathan cursed. The soft echo of his footsteps warned Lindsey of his approach, but she still jumped when he placed his hand on her shoulder. He lightly kneaded the tense muscles there before winding his arms around her in a loose embrace.

"Lindsey, I'm sorry." He spoke near her ear. "I admit that when I first came to you I was looking for someone to help me hunt down and kill this guy. I wanted revenge for Zach. For Sarah. For myself. For making me watch." Lindsey covered one of his hands with her own. "After being with you again, I realized I couldn't ask that of you. I couldn't put you in danger like that. The thought of losing you again..." His arms tightened around her. "It terrifies me."

Nathan kissed Lindsey's temple before gently turning her to face him. She kept her eyes closed as he brushed her damp cheeks. Not until he placed a finger under her chin and tipped it up did she meet his gaze.

"I'm sorry." Sincerity showed in his eyes, but Lindsey also saw a hard determination that frightened her.

"You still plan to kill him, don't you?"

"Yes."

Lindsey placed her hands against Nathan's chest and pushed him away. She ignored the flicker of hurt, and perhaps disappointment, that crossed his face as his arms fell away from her. "There has to be another way."

"I've tried to think of another alternative, but if there is one, I can't see it."

"Avoid him. Stop dreamstriding," she said, her voice dripping distaste over the last word.

"No." Nathan shook his head, frustration etched in his features. "We've talked about this enough that you should know that's not a viable solution. Besides, it leaves everyone else vulnerable."

"Maybe not." Lindsey looked down and said in a near whisper, "Lawrence thinks he's after me." Drawing a deep breath, she continued, "Lawrence says that the others are safe."

Nathan snorted. "Lawrence thinks. Lawrence says." Lindsey glared at Nathan as he mocked her. "Let's assume Lawrence knows what he's talking about. That his little flock is safe from the big bad wolf. What about anyone who isn't part of his group?" The image of the dreamstrider Lindsey had met in the woods, the one who had taken wolf form, rose in her mind, accompanied by uncertainty and worry. "What's to say that our psychopath won't go after them? Or what if..." Nathan's voice dropped into a lower register as he approached Lindsey. "What if he starts targeting others to draw you out?"

Lindsey's breath caught, and her eyes widened at the cruelty inherent in the question. "Don't try to put this on me. You dragged me into this." Nathan looked away but offered no apology. Lindsey crossed her arms and walked in a tight circle. She shot a penetrating look at him. "Am I right that you were coming to me for help because you don't think you can take him on your own?"

Nathan slid his hands into his back pockets and rocked back on his heels. "Yes."

"But you still plan to kill him."

Jaw clenched, he nodded, a short, sharp movement.

"How?"

Nathan crossed his arms and appeared distinctly uncomfortable. "I still need your help. I want you to teach me." He continued before she could voice her protest, "Help me get stronger so I can kill the bastard."

"You want *me* to teach *you*?" Lindsey threw her hands in the air in exasperation. "Are you nuts? I can barely remember anything. I have no control of what I do. I just react. How do you expect me to teach you?" Nathan started to respond, but Lindsey silenced him with a cold look. "Besides, I see little difference in handing you a loaded weapon knowing what you plan and pulling the trigger myself."

"*Dammit, Lindsey!*" Nathan's voice was like a thunderclap, causing her to flinch. "It's not like we can go to the police. The son of a bitch needs to die." He made an angry slash with his hand. "It's the only way to stop him. Only a dreamstrider can end this, and I'm willing to be that person. I can be that person if you'll help me."

"No."

Nathan bit back a curse. "He killed Sarah and probably Zach. You knew them. Did you know that? Do you remember them?"

Distressed, Lindsey swallowed and shook her head. "No, but killing him will not make it right. It won't bring them back."

He stepped past her and entered the studio. "Left on his own, what do you think he'll do? Do you really believe *he* will stop?" He stabbed a finger at the portrait and pushed on mercilessly. "Do you have any reason to think that? Has he ever stopped long enough to find out why he's doing this? How many times has he come after you now? Because I would already be dead by now if he wanted to kill me." Nathan returned and stood over her. Tears obscured her vision, blurring his features. "How many more times do you think you can handle being shot? Stabbed?" Lindsey blinked rapidly, and the tears cascaded down her cheeks. "How long before he kills you?" he asked, his voice tight. He placed his hands on her stiff shoulders. His thumbs stroked her neck. "Dreamstride with me. You remember more each time. Let me watch you teleport, shape-shift. Let me see how it's done."

Lindsey dropped her chin. A strained, genuine laugh escaped her as she shrugged off Nathan's touch. "That's it? That's your plan? Watch me to see how it's done?" She swiped at her cheeks. "Great. Just great." She sidestepped him to enter the studio, grabbing her purse off the table in the hallway as she went. She dug through her purse and found her phone.

"Lindsey?"

"There's a serious flaw with your plan, Nathan." She gestured toward the painting of herself. "You've obviously seen me do these things before, but you still haven't figured it out." She faced him, making no effort to hide her contempt. "How do you get around in the dreams, Nathan?"

"Walk. Or run. Maybe if I'm desperate I can manage flying low to the ground," he said. "Sometimes things just change around me while I move."

"How exactly is that different from what I do?" Lindsey asked, baffled by his response. "Nathan, not to go all Yoda-esque, but have you considered that dreamstriding, like dreaming, is in your head?" Nathan frowned. "You believe you can do it or you don't. There's no middle ground." She sighed and pulled up the contact list on her phone.

"Who are you calling?"

"A cab," she said, thankful to Makayla for insisting freshman year that Lindsey keep the numbers for a couple of cab companies in her phone for emergencies and situations like this, although neither of them could have envisioned a scenario quite like this one.

"Lindsey, wait, please." She looked up at him, her thumb hovering over the call button. "Let me take you home. Please, I won't talk to you any more about dreamstriding. We don't have to talk at all. Just, please, let me do this for you."

The pleading in his voice and eyes tore at her. She dropped her phone back into her purse. "Fine."

CHAPTER TWENTY-ONE

LINDSEY SAT DEEP in a booth with her back against the wall and her legs extended across the bench. An untouched cheeseburger and french fries grew cold on a plate at her elbow. Condensation pooled around the base of her glass and seeped away across the uneven surface. Her computer warmed her lap. After reading the same line for at least the fifth time, she tipped her head back, closed her eyes, and passed a hand over her face. She needed to finish the article and complete the assignment, but fatigue pulled at her.

The sudden clatter of silverware and the crash of a tray hitting the table startled her, and with a sharp intake of breath, she jerked her head away from the wall. Disoriented, she glanced around. The sight of geometric patterns dancing across her computer's screen caused her to groan and wonder how long she had slept. Removing the computer from her lap, Lindsey swung her legs around. She sat up straight and faced Makayla.

Her friend leaned forward, her forearms resting on either side of her customary salad. Her hands tapped an irregular rhythm on the table as she beamed at Lindsey. "*So?*"

Lowering her eyes, Lindsey pulled her cold lunch in front of her and dragged a fry through the ketchup. "So what?"

"What do you mean *so what*, Lindsey?" Makayla whined her name in exasperation. "So, Saturday night. Nathan. You went home with him. Come on. Spill already."

Lindsey met Makayla's expectant gaze and felt her stomach twist. She dropped the fry back onto her plate. "I'm trying not to think about it."

Makayla sagged in her seat. "Uh-huh." With narrowed eyes, she nodded sagely. "And I suppose working on..." She waved toward Lindsey's computer.

Lindsey obligingly filled in the blank. "Ento—" she began then amended, "my bug class."

"Yeah. Right." Makayla rolled her eyes. "And working on that is keeping you from thinking about Nathan? The god," Makayla concluded in a sultry growl.

"Yes."

"Really?" Makayla raised a brow and crossed her arms.

"Yes," Lindsey said, shifting in her seat. Unable to meet Makayla's knowing gaze any longer, she reached to wake the computer and bring up the article she had been reading. "Did you know that a nonnative tree species, even if it's been here for centuries, doesn't support nearly the same amount of fauna as it does in its native habitat."

"Fauna?"

"Insects, mostly."

"Really?"

"Mm-hmm." Lindsey forced herself to look at Makayla.

Makayla slumped forward and rested her chin on her hand.

A twinkle lit her eye and a grin teased at the corners of her mouth. "I thought Fauna was one of the good fairies in *Sleeping Beauty*."

Lindsey smiled.

Makayla tore open a packet of salad dressing and poured a sparing amount over her salad. "And how do they know that? About the bugs? Are they sending up some poor sap of an undergrad looking for extra credit up into the trees to count them?"

"I'm not sure, but I doubt it."

With a glint in her eye Makayla said, "Well, then, what about one of those things they use to pick fruit? You know, the things with the big metal clamps that grab the trunk." Makayla put her hands up in front of her. "And then they shake the tree really, really fast." She mimed the action. "And all the fruit falls off. I saw it on TV. On one of those how-it-works shows."

Lindsey grinned. "I don't think that would work on the flying things."

"Weeell…I suppose they could tent the tree and fumigate the whole thing. Might kill the tree, but the dead bugs would be worth it." Makayla nodded, and her eyes gleamed with satisfaction at the thought of bug corpses littering the ground.

Lindsey cringed. "God, I hope not."

Makayla shook her head and stabbed her salad. "Tell me again why you're spoiling a whole semester of lunches with bug talk."

"It fills a diversity requirement," Lindsey said, her tone flat with her often-repeated explanation.

"But you're pre-med," Makayla protested.

"I'm a bio major."

"Still, Lindsey, when are you going to need to know about bugs working in a hospital or an office?"

"Hospitals sometimes use leeches."

Makayla shuddered. "I so didn't need to know that."

"Besides, I'm not sure about the whole med school thing," Lindsey said.

Makayla froze and sent Lindsey a sharp look before turning to her salad and dragging her fork through it. "You know," she said, lifting her eyes to Lindsey's. "If student housing hadn't put us together freshman year, I doubt we would have ever crossed paths."

Lindsey held Makayla's gaze and gave the idea some thought. "Probably not."

"And I would have missed out on a great friend."

"Me too," Lindsey said, feeling a bit choked up.

"So how about telling me what happened?"

Lindsey sighed and pushed her food aside. She leaned forward against the table. Makayla followed her example. Pitching her voice low, Lindsey said, "Nathan asked me to do something I'm not comfortable with."

"Sex?" Makayla's eyebrows shot up. "Is he into kinky stuff?"

"No." Lindsey felt her cheeks redden and glanced around in embarrassment.

"Oh, I know," Makayla said. "A ménage à trois. Does he have a brother? No. Wait. That'd be too incestuous. No. How about..." She fell back against the seat, pulled her shirt from her chest, and fanned herself with it in quick up-and-down motions. "Imagine being sandwiched between him and Jason."

Wondering how a conversation could get so out of control so quickly, Lindsey buried her face in her hands as Makayla purred over the idea of a Jason-Nathan sandwich. "*No*, Makayla. No."

Almost looking disappointed, Makayla leaned forward again. "Okay, not sex. Drugs?"

Lindsey shook her head.

"Surely he hasn't already asked you to move in? Or elope? Or something?"

"No. No, nothing like that."

"Then what?"

Lindsey put her head on the table. When she spoke, her voice sounded hollow. "Makayla, it's complicated."

"No, Lindsey, it's not." Makayla touched her arm. "Just tell me what it is, and we'll figure it out."

Lindsey lifted her chin and saw the concern

clouding Makayla's eyes. "I can't talk here."

"Fine." Makayla started to slide out of the booth. "We'll go somewhere else."

"But you haven't finished your lunch."

"Neither have you. Besides," she added with a broad smile, "I'm bored with salads."

Lindsey and Makayla walked until they found a vacant bench near the library. At the rear of the building and slightly off the path, it offered a semblance of privacy. The cold from the stone penetrated Lindsey's jeans, but the sun shone brightly and kept her from getting uncomfortably cold.

Looking into the distance for fear of what she might see on her friend's face, Lindsey took a deep breath and began. She told Makayla about her childhood nightmares and meeting Nathan, how he had helped and comforted her. When Lindsey related Nathan's supposed death, Makayla sucked in a sharp breath and muttered, "Bastard." Lindsey paused, gratified by Makayla's response. As Lindsey explained about the changes in the dreams and the real source of her recent injuries, Makayla's fingers dug into Lindsey's arm. Haltingly, Lindsey recounted her conversation with Lawrence and her confrontation with Nathan the following morning. When she finished, silence descended, broken only by birdsong.

"You think I'm nuts, don't you?"

"No."

Surprised, Lindsey stared at Makayla. "You don't?"

"No." Makayla shook her head. Lifting a shoulder and giving Lindsey a half smile, she continued, "I'm not saying it's not a lot to take in, but, yeah, I believe you. And not that 'I believe that you believe' kind of believe, either." She patted Lindsey's hand. "You're sort of like a superhero when you do this dream stuff, aren't you? Special abilities and all that. You even have an evil nemesis."

Stunned by her friend's easy acceptance, it took Lindsey a moment to respond. "I can't say I've thought of it like that."

Makayla nodded and looked away. "It might help, though, if you did. Give yourself a little distance. Get a better perspective on the situation. Maybe find an answer. What would Wonder Woman do?"

"I have no idea," Lindsey said. "I've never read the comic."

Makayla flashed Lindsey a wide grin. "Me either. But I figured if we were going to invoke some inspiration, we should go for girl power."

She leaned to the side and bumped Lindsey's shoulder. "So, seriously, what are you going to do?"

Lindsey bit her lip and shook her head. "I don't know."

"You probably won't want to hear this." Makayla grasped Lindsey's hand. "But I think you should help Nathan."

Lindsey pulled away and started to protest.

"Wait," Makayla said. "Hear me out." She licked her lips and took a deep breath. "This guy who Nathan wants your help with—"

"Who Nathan wants to kill," Lindsey said, her voice cold.

"Fine. This guy who Nathan wants to kill. He sounds like a monster, and Nathan's right. It's not like the police can do anything about him. They don't even know that there's been a crime. It's going to take someone who can do this dream stuff that you guys can do to stop him."

"Makayla, I can't."

"But you don't have to. Just help Nathan power up."

"I'm not sure that I can, but even if I could, how is that any different? Ultimately, I'm still responsible." Lindsey dropped her gaze. She tamped down a patch of snow that had escaped the sun's rays and turned it into brown slush. "I just can't do it."

"So, what will you do?" Makayla asked, her tone gentle.

Lindsey shrugged. "Stop, if I can. If I can't, hide. If I can't hide, then run." She looked at Makayla with a sense of desperation. "He has to give up some time, right?"

"Maybe." Makayla's closed expression offered Lindsey no comfort. "What about Nathan?"

"Nathan." Lindsey buried her face in her hands. "How can we have a relationship when he's lied like he has? How can I trust him?"

"Yeah, I can't dispute you on that. He's been a stupid ass, but that's not where I was going." Lindsey lifted her head and looked at Makayla. "I get the feeling you've been pretty focused on the idea of killing this guy, but there's something else you need to consider. Will Nathan quit? Will he hide? Or run?"

A wave of unease washed over Lindsey. "I doubt it," she said. "He's pretty determined."

"So, he'll go after him."

"Yes."

"But he can't take this guy out."

"No." Lindsey began to shiver, and she admitted to herself it had nothing to do with the cold bench or the drop in temperature as the sun lowered to the horizon.

Makayla leaned close, her expression more intense than Lindsey was accustomed to seeing on her friend's face. "Lindsey, I'm not the one who will have to live with the consequences of whatever you decide, but will you be able to live with yourself if Nathan dies and there was a chance you could have prevented it?"

Wrapping her arms around herself, Lindsey swallowed past the lump in her throat. "No."

"You mentioned some other dream people—any chance that one of them might save you and Nathan the trouble?"

Lindsey shook her head. A tear fell unchecked, hot at first, then leaving a cold track down her cheek. "Lawrence." Lindsey cleared her throat and wiped at her cheek before continuing, "Lawrence won't do anything, and he's not telling any of his group what's going on. I can't blame him." Lindsey flashed a fragile smile. "I don't think any of them are strong enough, and so far they've been left alone."

Makayla rubbed Lindsey's back. "Can you take him?"

"Nathan thinks so."

Giving Lindsey's shoulder a light squeeze, Makayla asked, "What do you think?"

Lindsey contemplated Makayla's question. She struggled to consider her experiences in the dream realm, to look past the fear and panic and evaluate her abilities objectively. The answer frightened her. She whispered it: "I think we're pretty evenly matched."

CHAPTER TWENTY-TWO

LINDSEY STOOD ATOP her hill and waited, certain that Nathan would join her when he entered the dream realm. What she would say to him when he arrived was far less certain.

She looked around her self-constructed landscape, attuned to anything that might be amiss. Although returning here was a risk, it was preferable to endangering Lawrence's group by waiting in his garden. If dreamstriding once more became her norm, she would need to construct a new safe haven.

The wind stirred the tall grass. The accompanying susurrus heralded Nathan's arrival moments before the sense of his golden warmth reached her. Lindsey located the sensation and turned to face it, watching as the space blurred and twisted, lost its color, then reformed around him as he materialized in the dream. With arms crossed, Lindsey waited for him to get his bearings.

Looking wary, Nathan approached her. An odd, tickling itch crawled over her, through her. Recognizing it as Nathan's attempt to gauge her mood before speaking to her, she clenched her jaw and mentally swatted it away. To her satisfaction, he flinched.

Shamefaced, he offered an apology. "I'm sorry. You haven't returned my calls." He stopped a couple paces from her and slid his hands into his back pockets. "I wasn't sure you would come back."

She met his questioning gaze. "I wasn't either." She glanced up and noted the darkening sky. Opening her senses to her surroundings, she checked for other anomalies. Something niggled at the edge of her awareness, but it was faint and still distant. She returned her attention to Nathan. "We should go somewhere else."

His hand dropped to the sword that appeared at his side as he turned to survey their surroundings. "Is he coming?"

"Most likely," Lindsey said. "Something doesn't feel right, and he knows this place now." She ignored Nathan's grimace at the reminder. "I don't really have another place. At least, not one I can remember."

"Most of us only have one location that we identify with. He knows my diner." Nathan frowned. "Before here, there was another place that you used to go." She felt his hesitation humming in the space between them. "You may still have a strong-enough connection to it to be able to seal it off from the rest of the plane."

The wind grew chill. "Where?"

Nathan held out his hand. With trepidation, Lindsey took it. His warm fingers enveloped hers, and the connection between them flared, as strong as ever but now tainted by mistrust, sorrow, betrayal. Lindsey sought to pull away, but Nathan held firm. She saw the raw pain in his eyes before he closed them and turned his head aside.

A dim image took form in her mind, a shared memory with Nathan. Without conscious thought, she latched on to it and set to giving it shape. Her hill melted away in a muddy wash of color. Nathan anchored her in the maelstrom that arose around them, and bit by bit shapes emerged. A tree. A fence. An old toolshed half covered in ivy. Recognition took hold. "No! Not here."

In desperation, she struggled against Nathan, tried to pull free of him, but he drew her to him and held her to his chest. Entrapped by his embrace and entangled by their connection, her attempt to escape the dream failed. She punched at him with her free hand. Over his shoulder she saw their surroundings dim, and, despite Lindsey's hope that they would fade entirely, they solidified. Every detail in place, appearing exactly the same as it had four years ago, the scene of Nathan's supposed death.

She went slack in his arms. Her forehead fell to his shoulder. *How could you? Here, of all places?*

"I'm sorry," he said, but she felt the hollowness of the sentiment. He might be sorry for the pain he caused her, but, driven by his desire to stop the killer, he felt justified in whatever course of action he took.

In that moment, Lindsey hated Nathan.

He recoiled and released her, his expression grim. She turned her back on him and started walking with every intention of leaving this place behind her. She pulled up short when she reached a barrier. Stretching out a hand, she rested her fingertips against it, tested it. It was similar to Lawrence's but a cube rather than a sphere. It also lacked the cohesive strength of Lawrence's barrier, and she judged it something she could shatter should she choose to do so. Lindsey curled her hand and pulled it back to her chest.

When she had entered the dream tonight, she had planned on talking to Nathan, because Makayla was right. No matter how hurt and angry Lindsey felt, if Nathan came to harm, and there was a chance she could have prevented it, guilt would consume her. She had hoped to dissuade him from pursuing the killer, to convince him to hide or quit dreamstriding entirely, especially if she proved unable to teach him the skills he desired. She had set aside the multiple voice mails with the intent of addressing those questions here which was as close to face to face as she was willing to get.

Perhaps better than face to face. She glanced over her shoulder at him again. Here she had a better chance of keeping him honest.

"I won't lie to you," he said.

Squaring her shoulders, Lindsey returned to him. "Forgive me if I have trouble believing that."

"I suppose I deserve that." His jaw tensed. A hint of anger simmered in his eyes and tinged the space around him. "But how many times am I supposed to apologize, Lindsey?"

"Until I believe you or get tired of hearing it," she snapped. Their surroundings darkened and cooled. "Let's be clear, Nathan." She stepped over to him and poked him in the chest.

Her voice a low growl, she continued, "I'm the injured party here. I'm the one who was deceived and manipulated. I'm only here now to make sure I have no regrets later. Got it?"

He nodded as he retreated beyond her reach.

"So then...bringing us here." She waved her hand around. "Which one of us did that?"

"You. I only provided the image."

Standing akimbo, Lindsey dropped her gaze to the ground. She chewed on her lower lip. "Would you say I teleported us here?"

"Yes."

"And you can't do that?" she asked, looking at him through narrowed eyes.

"I—I can..."

"But?"

He crossed his arms in front of his chest. "I'm slow at it, and I can only go places I've been before. Otherwise, I'm stuck with wandering around. You can go anywhere. Whether you've been there or not."

Lindsey turned in a tight circle and considered his supposition. Was he right? She recalled all the places she had passed through during her flight from her hill; they had been unknown to her until she arrived. Now the question was how did she do it. "I wasn't aiming for a place. I was just pushing myself from where I was at the moment."

"I'm sorry?"

Lindsey pinned Nathan with her gaze. "In an emergency, don't worry about the destination, just push away from where you are."

Nathan's brow furrowed. "Push how?"

"Will yourself away to somewhere else and don't bother with where that somewhere else is."

He shook his head. "I don't understand. How—"

"Nathan." Lindsey threw her hands up in exasperation. "There isn't a how. Want it to happen. Make it happen." She buried her face in her hands. "You know, I would have thought that I would be the one to overthink this stuff, not you." Lowering her hands, Lindsey said, "Okay. Forget teleporting. What else? What do you think I can teach you?"

"Shape-shifting," he said, his tone and eyes flat, betraying none of the frustration that splintered the space around him.

Lindsey looked away. She slowly turned and crossed to the barrier as her mind struggled to put a logical progression to how she altered her form, but, in the end, it came down to desire and will. With a sigh, she moved toward Nathan. "I can't explain it. Half the time, it's not even a conscious decision." Lindsey started to reach for him then stopped herself, letting her hand fall back to her side. "I can't teach you these things. I just do them. There's no step-by-step instruction that I can give you. If you want to teleport, then teleport. If you want to change shape, then do it." Nathan's jaw clenched. He pivoted and stalked away. "Please, let this go. Stop dreamstriding before you get yourself killed."

"No." The dream rippled around Nathan as he abruptly turned to face Lindsey. "I will not walk away from this. He needs to be stopped. I will find a way."

"But—"

"But," a smooth, deep voice echoed, sending chills through Lindsey. "How do you plan to stop him?"

She spun around, senses sweeping the area, searching for the source. Then, she saw him and froze.

"Especially when he can hold you still, and you can do nothing about it?" He stood behind Nathan's rigid form.

"Lindsey," the man purred. With a cold, brittle smile, he rested his chin on Nathan's left shoulder and reached over the right to drape his arm across Nathan's chest, resting his hand over

Nathan's heart. A blade glinted in his other hand as he tapped the flat of it against Nathan's leg. "She doesn't look happy to see me, does she?" His voice dropped as he spoke in Nathan's ear. Nathan's gaze never wavered from Lindsey's, and while she caught only disjointed fragments of what Nathan's captor said, she could see the emotions his words provoked. Anger. Frustration. Outrage. Despair.

"Let him go," Lindsey said, forcing the words past her fear. The man's attention snapped to her. She took a step toward them, intent on wresting Nathan free.

"Uh-uh." He pressed the blade to Nathan's abdomen, angling it up. "None of that."

She held up her hands, signaling her compliance and pleading for him to stop. The edges of her vision began to blur. "It's me you want. Not Nathan. Right?"

"True." He smiled, soft and genuine, and, to her confusion, affection shadowed his eyes before he closed them. His arm tightened around Nathan, whose muscles bunched and tightened with his futile efforts to escape.

"Tell me, Lindsey, if I release Nathan, what will you do?" He caught her in a cold, assessing gaze. "Will you stay? Will you give me the fight I want?" The dream wavered. Lindsey felt it, and, based on the way he glanced around, she guessed that he did too. He shook his head. "No. You can't." Determination settled over his features. "Not without sufficient motivation."

Before Lindsey could protest, he sank the blade into Nathan's chest. Her breath caught in her throat, and she fell to her knees. The agony engraved on Nathan's face filled her vision. His mouth and throat worked but no sound emerged, sealed within by the will of his captor. "Hush, now. I know it hurts, but we can't have you screaming and startling Lindsey out of the dream. We barely have her here with us as it is." Nathan's eyes fell closed, tears leaking from them. "Shh, it'll be over soon."

Lindsey felt the world around her losing substance and sliding away from her. Her vision narrowed to encompass Nathan, with the growing stain forming around the blade in his chest, and the monster who held him.

"Lindsey, look at me." She heard the firm, patient command but found herself unable to follow it. "Lindsey." Her name cracked around her with physical force, bringing the world back into sharp focus and forcing her to meet the man's gaze. "You know what I want."

She swallowed hard and nodded.

"This wound." He shifted the blade slightly, causing Lindsey to cringe as a moan escaped Nathan and fresh blood flowed. "It's deep. It's doing damage, but it's not fatal. Not yet." The space around the two men began to distort. "But there are limits to what any of us can endure." Black flames edged in electric blue appeared to wrap around them.

"No." Lindsey stretched a hand toward them. "Please."

"Find me. Give me what I want, and you might save him." The flames flared.

The men were gone.

CHAPTER TWENTY-THREE

"NATHAN." LINDSEY BOLTED upright in bed. The sheets clung to her damp body. Her breath came in short, shuddering gasps. She pushed her hair away from her face. Peeling back the sheets, she lurched onto unsteady legs and scrambled down the hall. With a trembling hand, she grabbed her phone from the counter, scrolled through the contacts, and called Nathan.

"Please pick up. Please hear me. Please tell me he can't keep you there." She squeezed her eyes tight and chewed the inside of her cheek as she listened to the phone ring. When it switched to voice mail, she whimpered. She sank to the floor and tried again. Her eyes burned with tears as she listened to the voice mail pick up again for the second, the third, the fourth time.

"Damn you, Nathan. Wake up and answer the phone." She made one more unsuccessful attempt then climbed to her feet. As she returned to her bedroom, she called a different number.

"Makayla? It's Lindsey. I know it's late. I'm so sorry, but I need your help."

Lindsey paced up and down the hall, coat on, purse bumping into her hip with every step. She peered through the peephole every time she reached the door, desperate for Makayla to arrive. Hearing a car on the street, she rushed to the door. Recognizing Makayla's car, Lindsey was out the door before Makayla could turn off the engine.

"I can't thank you enough," she said as she dove into Makayla's car.

"Anything for you. You've got his address?"

"Yes."

"The GPS is in the glove box."

Lindsey opened the compartment. "You'll need to go west on the highway."

"Got it." Makayla made a sharp left.

The glow of the GPS lit the interior of the car. While the device booted up, Lindsey blew on her fingers, warming them. She entered Nathan's address then attached the device to the windshield as Makayla merged onto the highway. Reaching into her pocket, Lindsey withdrew her phone, found Nathan's number, and pressed "send." His voice mail answered again. She closed her eyes and rested her head on the cold window.

"Still no answer?" Makayla said.

Lindsey shook her head. "No."

"Have you called nine-one-one?"

"And tell them what?"

"I don't know," Makayla said. "Lie. Tell them you were talking, and he said he heard a noise, and then he wasn't there but the connection was still good."

Lindsey fidgeted and rolled her phone from one hand to the other. "That sounds like something that could get us into a lot of trouble."

"Lindsey." Makayla shot her a look of disbelief. "The last time you saw Nathan, he had a piece of metal sticking out of his chest and was being dragged off by a psychopath. I wouldn't worry too much about getting into trouble right now."

"No, you don't understand," Lindsey said.

"Understand what?"

"But you've given me an idea. Something close to the truth." Lindsey's thumb ran over the keypad.

A dispatcher answered after the second ring.

"Nine-one-one. This call is being recorded. What's the nature of your emergency?"

"I've been trying to reach my boyfriend, but he isn't answering his phone or responding to messages. He was complaining of chest pains earlier today."

"Turn here," Lindsey said, although it was hardly necessary. Garish red and white lights flashed atop an ambulance and fire engine, reflecting off the snow and setting the neighborhood alight. As Makayla parked, a police car pulled around her. Its blue lights merged with the red and white in a kaleidoscopic effect.

As Lindsey slid out of the car, she watched the policemen approach the firemen who stood clustered in front of Nathan's home. A helmeted fireman broke from the group. Carrying a long tool that looked like a cross between a crowbar and a pickax, he climbed Nathan's front steps. He set the tool to the doorframe, and the sound of splintering wood carried through the cold air.

Makayla came to Lindsey's side and placed an arm around her waist. With numb detachment, Lindsey allowed Makayla to lead her to the house. The scene felt more surreal than anything she had encountered in dreams.

The fireman backed away from the door. He lifted the tool and swung it at the doorjamb. It hit with a solid thunk. He leaned on the long handle, pushing it toward the door. With a squeak and a cracking groan that made Lindsey cringe, the door opened. The EMS team filed through as soon as it was clear.

"I'll be right back," Makayla said, patting Lindsey's arm.

Lindsey nodded absently, her attention fixed on the house, watching the lights come on as the EMS team moved through the interior. When she registered Makayla's voice saying *girlfriend*, Lindsey looked for her friend and saw her talking to one of the firemen. She saw him nod and heard his rumbling bass but could not make out his words.

With an air of determination, Makayla returned to Lindsey, took her by the hand, and started for the house. "Come on. He said we could go in as long as we stayed calm and out of the way. Let's go see how bad this is."

With a mixture of gratitude to Makayla and trepidation at what awaited them, Lindsey trailed after her friend, quickening her pace as they drew near the house then fairly flying up the steps once they were inside. She drew up short at Nathan's bedroom door, stopping just beyond the threshold.

He lay on the bed. The paramedic team, a man and a woman, bent over him. Lindsey saw the man insert something into Nathan's mouth as his partner attached something to Nathan's wrists. Lindsey snatched glances of Nathan's face between the paramedics' quick and efficient movements. Could they see it? Not knowing Nathan, did they realize? "He's so pale."

The woman looked up. "You know him."

Lindsey nodded and wrapped her arms around herself.

"Is he on any medications?" She attached leads to Nathan's chest while her partner started an IV.

"No. I don't think so."

"Does he have any allergies?"

"He hasn't mentioned any."

The woman acknowledged Lindsey with a terse nod. Her partner moved to Nathan's ankles and attached two leads, completing a fine network of wires.

"Excuse me," a male voice said from behind Lindsey. Makayla grabbed her arm and steered her back out of the room. A pair of firemen entered, bringing a stretcher with them. A barely discernible beeping emanated from within.

"There's ST elevation," Lindsey heard the

woman say. The phrase meant nothing to Lindsey, but the team's demeanor told her it was not good. She felt her throat closing. She bit her lip and blinked back tears. She turned to Makayla and said in a soft, choked voice, "I need to get out of here."

"Okay, Linds," Makayla said with a worried look at her and a last concerned glance at Nathan.

Lindsey led the way down the stairs and out of the house. A crushing sense of responsibility weighed on her even though she knew that the situation was not of her making and not her fault. Still, she needed to fix it if she could. She stopped on Nathan's lawn. Makayla set her hand between Lindsey's shoulders and began to rub her back in small circles.

The EMS team soon emerged from the house. One of them separated from the others and walked toward Lindsey. "You can ride up front if you like."

"No, thank you."

He accepted her answer and rejoined the crew.

"Lindsey, are you sure?" Makayla asked, wrapping a comforting arm around her friend.

Lindsey watched as the EMS team loaded Nathan into the ambulance. The woman who had connected the leads and one of the firemen climbed into the back of the truck. The other paramedic closed the doors behind them.

"Should we follow them?"

"No. I can't help Nathan there." Lights flashing, the ambulance pulled away from the curb. It drove down the street and turned the corner. Its lights continued to fill the sky, allowing Lindsey to briefly track its passage. The fire engine soon followed it while the police cruiser remained behind.

"Take me home," Lindsey said, her breath clouding around her in the cold air.

Makayla shifted and Lindsey could feel her gaze. "You're sure?"

A siren sounded in the distance, and Lindsey wondered if it was the ambulance transporting Nathan. She ground her teeth together and swallowed past the tightness in her throat. With a curt nod, she separated from Makayla and returned to the car.

The two drove in silence until they neared Lindsey's apartment. "Lindsey, what are you planning?"

"I'm going to get Nathan."

"Won't he be okay now? He's in a hospital."

Lindsey looked at Makayla, caught the worried glance she sent her. "I would like to think so, but I can't make myself believe it." She looked out the passenger-side window, watching as the oaks went by, silent sentries leading her home. "If it's just the one wound, maybe, but if Nathan's stabbed again—repeatedly—can they keep up? Find it in time? Prevent permanent damage?" She shook her head, grim determination settling over her. "No, I need to go get him."

Makayla stopped in front of Lindsey's home and cut the engine. The windows began to fog. "I don't like this, Linds."

"Neither do I." Lindsey looked at Makayla. "But what else can I do?"

Makayla leaned over and pulled Lindsey into a tight hug. "Be careful."

Lindsey squeezed Makayla tight, nodded against her shoulder, and got out of the car.

Once inside, she checked the clock. It was only two a.m. How could so much have happened already? Still plenty of hours to sleep before the world would start to awaken and create a low hum of activity that could interfere, and he would undoubtedly be waiting for her return. Lindsey went to the kitchen. Wanting to be sure she stayed asleep as long as necessary, she swallowed four pills. She then settled into her bed and waited for the antihistamine to help her fall asleep.

CHAPTER TWENTY-FOUR

LINDSEY FOCUSED ON the place where she had last seen Nathan, but, despite it being based on her childhood backyard, returning there proved difficult. She struggled against dark memories and the most recent trauma that tainted the place in her mind and made her instinctively wish to avoid it. Only her determination to find some sign that would lead her to Nathan allowed her to shape the void and hold it stable.

Turning in place, Lindsey examined the area. Everything seemed in order, but she sensed no other dreamstriders nearby. Despondently, she walked to where Nathan had last stood. There was no sign of him or the one who had taken him. No evidence or clue as to where they were or if Nathan still lived.

Lindsey clenched her fists and scowled.

Now what was she supposed to do? How did you find someone in a place shaped by thoughts, memories, and imaginings? If she viewed this place the way Lawrence had shown her, would she recognize the space claimed by the monster?

Tilting back her head, she studied the blue sky above. She allowed herself a brief moment of imagining that she was here for no other purpose than to take to the heights and soar in the vast expanse above. Closing her eyes, she hung her head. No flying tonight: she needed to find Nathan as he had found her.

She stiffened. Her eyes opened wide. The link Nathan had forged between them with one of her feathers—could she use it? Chewing on her thumb, Lindsey began to pace. She had been unaware of it until he pulled on it. Even now, knowing it existed, it remained outside of her perception. If she could contact Nathan, would he be able to activate it? Undoubtedly, he was being held where he was, but could he reel her in to him?

Bracing herself, Lindsey stood still. She imagined her voice carrying across the dream realm, to all the spheres Lawrence had shown her and all the shadowed places in between. She drew in a deep breath and called, "Nathan." The force of her will created a wave that rippled out from her, distorted the world around her, and announced her presence to all.

An icy blast hit her from behind. She whirled, raising a hand and blocking a blow on the dagger she willed into being. She followed through with the other hand and another dagger, nearly plunging it into her attacker's side before he jumped back. He crouched low before her, his arms raised before him, a blade held in each hand. His eyes gleamed laserlike over the sharp edges.

Lindsey mirrored his posture as they sized each other up. She caught a glimpse of his cold grin as he launched another attack. She countered his blows with a flurry of forearm on forearm and metal on metal. Their fighting moved too quickly to give her time to think, forcing her to react on instinct alone. As she parried with one blade, she spied an opening and lunged, drawing blood along his ribs.

With a yelp and look of shock he pulled back. His hand dipped to his side. His fingers came away red. Lindsey felt her lips pull back in a feral grin. The bastard wanted a fight and she would give it to him. With a huff of laughter, he mock-saluted her with one dagger before he stepped back into an explosion of blue and black and disappeared.

Lindsey's sense of triumph at drawing first blood fled. She stared in disbelief at the space he had vacated. He had run away, and she was no closer to rescuing Nathan. With a growl of frustration, she hurled one of the daggers at the shed. *Thunk.* It hit the side, the blade biting into the wood siding.

She studied the short blade she still held, turned it, and spied a trace of blood along its length. Nathan had used one of her bloody feathers to create the link between them: could she do the same to her attacker?

Biting her lower lip at the possible repercussions of what she was about to do, Lindsey brought the blade to her mouth. Clamping down on the voice of caution, she placed her tongue on the cool metal above the guard. She shuddered at the contact. Slowly, she ran her tongue along the length of the blade. Her eyelids lowered until they nearly closed as she tasted her prey. When she reached the tip, she drew in her tongue and sucked on her lower lip, consuming every trace of him that she could. She closed her eyes and rode a wave of euphoria before a montage of images and emotions flashed through her mind.

Lawrence had been correct about the man

wanting to die. She felt his desperation. But, she also felt his fear.

She exhaled through parted lips. Opening her eyes the merest crack, she discerned a gossamer thread of oily black stretching into the distance. The corner of her mouth quirked with a half smile. She eased the dagger into the sheath that she willed to appear on her thigh, and then she focused on the thread. A subtle tension built in her abdomen and her muscles tightened in response to the pull of the ghastly umbilical cord. Stretching out a hand, she summoned her other blade. The hilt slapped her palm, and she sheathed it as she contemplated her options.

The cord connected her to her prey, but it gave her no sense of distance or location. She knew she would find him at the other end, but would Nathan be there as well? With pursed lips and a furrowed brow, she began to follow the path. If she pulled herself along its length, what would she find? Would there be a moment of disorientation that would leave her open and vulnerable to attack? Lindsey paused. Better not to risk it, but simply following the trail would not suffice either. Even with medical support, Nathan's time was limited.

Narrowing her eyes, she focused on the farthest point of the thread that she could see. She pictured her hand wrapping around it, grasping it firmly, and pulled. Her surroundings passed by in a blur, and she stumbled when she suddenly halted, tripping over both feet. After regaining her bearings, Lindsey took ahold of the cord once more. She simultaneously pulled and stepped forward. Her foot hit the ground as she reached her target, leaving her a bit unsteady but nowhere near as bad. With a pleased smile, she repeated the process. With every step, it became smoother and easier. Soon she moved with the natural fluidity of walking.

When the cord led her to a train station on the outskirts of a rundown city, Lindsey stopped. The gossamer strand followed the tracks, curving into the distance and disappearing among the buildings. The increased tension in her abdomen suggested that she was close to her goal, but, lacking a clear line of sight, her current method of pursuit would be ineffective. She ground her teeth in frustration and fought the temptation to close the distance with one blind pull. She walked to the edge of the platform, prepared to jump onto the tracks and traverse their length if that was what it took. The rattle of an approaching train gave her pause. As it rumbled past her with a hot gust of wind, she decided against walking the tracks.

With a glance at the grey sky, she considered changing shape and flying. From the air she might be able to see the thread well enough to find a direct route, but she would be unable to defend herself from whatever weapons he might wield. She raised her hand to her left shoulder, remembering the pain of being shot. Did she really want to be in another form when she caught up with her prey?

The sound of another train approaching drew her attention. This one traveled in the direction of the cord. The brakes squealed as it slowed and came to a stop before her. Its doors slid open in invitation.

Cautiously, senses alert for any abnormalities, she approached the car. She peered around the door. The cord rested on the floor, leading to the front of the train. She boarded, and the doors closed behind her. Catching sight of something with her peripheral vision, she turned and faced her own reflection in the window of the door. She stared, surprised by how different she appeared from the way she normally pictured herself. The woman who looked back at her was sleek and fierce, a warrior primed for battle. It rattled her, but at the same time she felt empowered.

Casting a glance at the cord to make certain the train indeed followed the same path, Lindsey lowered herself onto one of the seats. The car rattled and rocked as it moved. Somnolence clawed at her, but she remained focused on her goal, monitoring the cord's tension.

The train dipped down and entered a tunnel that amplified the sound of the train's passing. It went dark save for a faint blue luminescence emanating from the thread. Lindsey braced herself against the possibility of being attacked. For a brief terrifying moment, everything slowed and grew heavy, and then the train exited the tunnel. Lindsey caught her breath at the changes in her surroundings.

Graffiti filled the interior of the car, and trash littered the floor, stirring and shifting in the gusts of air that entered through the gaping holes that pocked the roof. Red tinted the now-visible sky. Dark clouds roiled across it, lightning jumping between them. The train jerked and turned sharply. An alarming groan sounded from above. Raising her arms protectively over her head, Lindsey curled into a tight ball as large portions of the roof collapsed. The wind carried away much of the debris, but shards of sharp metal still rained around her, slicing her arms. When nothing more fell, she stood up and assessed the damage. With gritted teeth, she pulled a sliver out of her arm. As she tossed the two-inch fragment to the floor, she realized the cord was no longer there.

She spun around. Focusing on the tight knot in her abdomen, she sought the connection she had forged. It still thrummed there, but when she tried to envision it, no thread appeared. Instead, the world around her pulsed. Taking a wide stance against the motion of the train, she craned her neck back to face the sky. She closed her eyes. When she opened them again, she saw the world as Lawrence had shown it to her, saw the dense dome, and understood. She moved within her prey's sphere.

She was near, and he would know it. He would know that she was coming for him.

She blinked and the world returned to its more familiar construct. The warm flow of blood down her fingertips recalled her attention to her wounded arm. She pushed up her soaked sleeve and examined it. Running her hand over the wound, she imagined the skin whole and unbroken, but it remained unchanged; Lindsey stared at her arm in disbelief. She pictured gauze strips wrapping around it and watched in irritation as they appeared and wove around the injured area with the meticulous precision of a spider weaving a web. Determining why one thing worked and not the other was a puzzle for another time. She gave her arm a quick shake, and her sleeve dropped back into place.

The train slowed to a stop and the doors parted. Drawing one of the daggers, Lindsey exited, stepping out not onto a train platform but a sidewalk. Directly before her was a flight of stairs leading to an old brownstone.

The building stood in stark contrast to its derelict neighbors. It appeared clean and well maintained, its windows still intact. Flowers grew in the window boxes, and draped over the balustrade was a faded quilt in blue and white.

Suppressing a rush of nerves, Lindsey climbed the steps. The door swung open under her touch. She stretched her senses, alert for any changes in her surroundings, then crossed the threshold. Blade held at the ready, she traversed a short hallway until it opened into a large space with dark wood floors and white walls. A pair of Queen Anne chairs and a settee upholstered in vivid red furnished the room, arranged in front of a brick fireplace that someone had had the bad taste to paint white. Empty sconces flanked it.

She edged into the room and took a broader view. Gauzy sheers danced in a gentle breeze save for one panel that billowed like a sail, its bottom edge trapped under Nathan's recumbent form. Tightening her grip on her knife, she strode toward him, hesitating only briefly at the chill that brushed the nape of her neck. She ignored the sound of slow clapping and the soft tread of her prey as he trailed her. This close to him, bound as they now were, she could decipher his moods almost as well as she could decipher Nathan's in this place. He had no intention of attacking her. Not yet.

She stepped over Nathan's legs and pushed aside the loose curtains. She lowered herself next to him and carefully removed the corner of the bloodstained trapped panel from underneath his arm.

"I expected you sooner."

Grinding her teeth, Lindsey gave her nemesis a dark look and met steel-grey eyes that were partially obscured by tousled black locks. "Have I disappointed you"—she shoved the bloodied curtain aside—"*Dominic?*"

She caught his look of surprise before she turned to study Nathan's drawn features. He looked so pale, his normally golden-brown complexion now ashen. His chest barely moved. She took his hand, expecting their connection to flare. Nothing happened. *Nathan.* No response.

"I suspect it's too late." Dominic squatted opposite Lindsey and poked Nathan in the shoulder.

She shook her head. "No. He's still here, and I got him to a hospital." Feeling Dominic's mood shift, Lindsey tensed.

"You know him outside?"

"He found me," she said, meeting his stormy gaze.

Radiating weariness, Dominic looked at Nathan. He adjusted his position, resting one knee on the ground. He placed the heel of his right hand on Nathan's sternum, bracketing the blade between his thumb and other fingers. With his left, he took the hilt in hand. "If you have any goodbyes to say, you should say them now." He pulled on the dagger. It caught and met resistance, and then it was free. Blood welled from the open wound until Dominic ran his hand over it.

Lindsey felt a twinge of self-disgust that Dominic should be able to so easily seal the wound while all she had managed was mummy wrappings for herself. Biting her lip, she waited for Nathan to leave the dream. When he continued to remain, she shot a hostile look at Dominic. With grim amusement, he stood, his mouth twisted in a thin, lopsided smile.

"I've let go. Now you have to, too," he said with a pointed glance at her hand holding Nathan's.

The thought of releasing Nathan sent a wave of panic through her. True, he was unconscious and unable to help her, but he was here and his presence lent a degree of comfort and security. Once he left the dream realm, she would be alone with Dominic. Despite his calm demeanor, violence and determination simmered deep inside him, awaiting a trigger. Nathan's disappearance might be that trigger.

Holding Dominic's gaze, Lindsey let her fingers slide out of Nathan's slack grip and got to her feet. She felt Nathan slip from the dream. His absence created a brief vacuum in the fabric of her perception, and she resisted the urge to look down and study the spot where he had lain.

"You have my name. Does it have anything to do with this?" Dominic cupped his hand in front of himself at waist level, and a heavy silver rope appeared within it, draping between them. He rocked his wrist and set the cord to swaying. "Is this how you found me?"

"Yes."

"Clever bit of work. Mind if I ask how you did it?"

"It's something I learned from Nathan."

"Really?" Dominic's eye dropped to the cord. "So he had a hidden skill after all," he said with a slight smile. He turned back to Lindsey with an air of expectation about him. The cord swung in lazy loops like a jump rope.

Lindsey raised one of her daggers. "You left a bit of yourself behind." She pointed to his side. "I used that."

Dominic stopped swinging the cord. It fell flat at the top of its arc. It continued to ripple and sway before hanging limp. "Blood."

She nodded.

He dropped the cord and it faded from sight. "You didn't hesitate to tell me. No worries that I'll use the technique on someone? You mean to follow this through, don't you?"

"If necessary."

His lips drew back in a savage grin. He slid a foot back, taking a wider stance, and crouched low with one hand held in front of him. A short sword appeared in his other hand; he stood with it positioned down and back, poised to strike. "Come on, then. Summon that pretty blade I saw Nathan give you and let's go."

Lindsey tilted her head as she parsed his meaning. The image of a slender rapier floated before her. She closed her eyes against it and shook her head. "It no longer suits me." She brought her hands up, a blade in each. "We don't need to do this."

He snorted. "You delved deep enough to find my name. Surely, you know better."

"I know you want to die. I also know you're scared."

Dominic's eyes hardened. His blade dipped. "Enough."

He sprang at Lindsey. Instead of meeting his attack, she teleported and occupied the space he had vacated. Taking a defensive stance, she faced Dominic as he whirled around. With a mixture of irritation and delight, he came at her again. She teleported again, a brief flickering motion that moved her a few feet to the side. Believing that she had dodged his attack, she prepared to repeat the maneuver, but a sudden weight slammed into her, knocking her off her feet. Burning pain shot through her arm. A quick glance showed blood soaking her sleeve.

Dominic stood over her and tasted his bloodied blade. The cord between them pulsed. "No more jumping around, Lindsey. No more running away." She climbed to her feet. "Fight me. Or die."

Resolve wrapped around Lindsey, sank into her bones. When Dominic attacked, she met him head on. They came together and broke apart. They spun and circled each other in a deadly dance. Each sustained injuries. Their blood dripped onto the floor, making it slick. Their feet slid and smeared the blood until the floor resembled a Jackson Pollock painting. Chests heaving, the combatants separated and reassessed the situation.

Numerous cuts covered Lindsey's arms and legs, yet not once had Dominic struck her torso, and not for lack of opportunity. She did not deceive herself on that point. Just as she had passed on openings, so had he. "You don't want to kill me any more than I want to kill you. Let's end this."

He shook his head. "You're right." In a sudden blue-tinged blur, he appeared in front of Lindsey and grabbed her by her shirt. Her feet left the ground as he continued his forward motion. Her back slammed against the wall, knocking the breath from her. He leaned down until they were nose to nose. "But make no mistake." Cold metal kissed her cheek. "I *will* kill you, if you don't kill me." With a vicious twist, he rotated the blade from flat to edge and laid open her cheek down to the bone.

She screamed. Dropping her daggers, she flailed against him, desperate to escape him and the dream, but despite the pain and sudden on-slaught of terror, she remained anchored within it. Dominic flung her from him, casting her across the room. She landed hard on her hip and rolled until she came up against the settee.

Sprawled on her back, she tested her cheek with an unsteady hand and sucked in a breath through her teeth at the contact. Hearing the floor creak, she turned her head and saw Dominic approaching. Keeping watch on him, she lifted her right arm and leg across her battered body, forcing it to roll. Then she hoisted herself onto her other elbow and knee and perched awkwardly on all fours. With Dominic looming over her, she curled her toes toward her shins, shifted her weight to the balls of her feet, and placed one hand on the settee. Dominic raised his sword, and Lindsey lunged at him.

She hit him low in the hips, knocking him off balance. Their bodies tangled and headed for the floor. The hilt of his sword struck a glancing blow across her back. More angered than hurt by the contact, she growled low in her throat. They crashed onto the wood floor. He abandoned his sword and grabbed at her. She twisted within his grasp.

In her struggle to break free, she jarred her mutilated cheek. She let her pain and blind fury flow through her, then reshape her with a familiar push-pull sensation. When the light that briefly engulfed her receded, she stretched tawny front paws out and sank her claws into the wood. Powerful shoulder muscles flexed. Strong hind legs bunched and clawed, freeing her of the one who had tried to hold her. She leapt away and spun around to face him. Her tail whipped with her rage. Her lips drew back with a snarl, revealing her fangs.

She watched him climb to his feet. Pleasure suffused her at the sight of the gouge marks along his legs. On padded feet, she circled him, stalked him. With heavy, unsteady steps, he turned and glared at her with an animosity that rivaled her own. Between strides, wrapped in a soft glow, she altered form again, abandoning four paws for two legs, claws for sharp blades, but the desire to destroy her prey remained.

Dominic stooped to retrieve his sword, and she attacked. Though off balance, he respond-ed with surprising speed and blocked her strike. She followed through with her other blade. The sound of grating metal filled the space as he met her blade with one of his own. His short sword shrank to a size more suited for close combat, and the pair went at each other with full force.

The bond forged by her and reinforced by

him pulsed between them with the shared joy at finding an opponent of equal strength and skill. Neither held back; no opening was ignored. Both bled from multiple wounds. Exhilaration fueled them, smothering fatigue and dampening pain.

She feinted. He fell for the ploy, leaving his chest exposed. She stabbed at the opening and impaled him on her blade, burying it to the hilt.

Triumph coursed through Lindsey. She cried out in victory, and then she met Dominic's eyes, wide with shock. The sight of blood bubbling from between his lips turned her cold. His knees buckled, and he drew her down with him. What had she done? With hands slippery from exertion and blood, she gripped the dagger. Dominic stayed her hand, covering it with his own.

No.

"But it's not too late."

A pained smile curved his lips, and he choked out laughter. *It's two years too late.*

Memories came unbidden through their bond. Dominic playing football, tackling a quarterback and halting the opposing team's last-minute drive down the field. Dominic celebrating an athletic scholarship to his first-choice university. Dominic taking a hit during training camp, falling to the ground with no feeling from the neck down. Dominic bedridden, surrounded by trophies of better days, emaciated, dependent on a machine to breathe. *I can't even wipe my own ass.*

Tears streaked Lindsey's cheeks, cutting watery pink tracks through the blood. She searched for words of comfort, consolation, hope, but they all felt empty when faced with the depth of his grief. She sought to send him a sense of encouragement.

I don't want your pity. His anger burned her. She saw the faces of his friends and teammates who had visited regularly at first, then drifted away into their own lives. The few who had remained constant, Dominic drove away, unable to take what he believed was pity masked by false cheer.

He coughed, drawing her back to the present. She studied him. His breathing came in wet rasps. His pallid complexion reminded her of Nathan. She dropped her gaze to where her hand still wrapped around the hilt and felt nauseated. She had to stop this.

Anger flared in his eyes and through the bond. His hand convulsed around hers. His other hand whipped up and wrapped around the back of her neck, forcing her closer. "No!

Finish it." He bullied his way into her mind and pillaged her memories for images of those she held dear. *Everyone comes here sooner or later. Lose your resolve now and I will hunt them all down, starting with Lawrence and his flock, Nathan if he survives, all of them, and I will make sure you live to witness all of it.*

She shook her head in denial and trembled in the wake of his assault. Her forehead fell against his. "Please."

Stay with me. Hold me until the end. I can't do this anymore.

Lindsey succumbed to the bitter poison of his self-loathing. She tightened her grip on the hilt. She held him in the dream when he would have woken from it.

His hand slipped from the back of her neck. He ran it over her open cheek, soothing the pain as he sealed it. He pressed his cheek to her temple and spoke in her ear. "Thank you."

His hand dropped to his side. She squeezed her eyes shut tight and bit her lip. She felt his presence fade and his body become nothing more than a hollow afterimage of her own creation.

CHAPTER TWENTY-FIVE

LINDSEY OPENED HER eyes and stared unseeing at the ceiling. Tears ran down her temples past her ears, wetting her hair and the pillow below. A hard lump lodged in her throat. She began to tremble. Her stomach clenched. She rolled to her side and swallowed hard against the rising wave of nausea.

Midway through drawing back the blankets, a cold prickling sensation crawled across her scalp as she perceived a dark shape near the bathroom. She blinked in confusion as her eyes adjusted to the dim light. Fear settled over her when she realized that a man sat there with his legs bent, head tipped back against the wall, watching her.

"It's all right," he said, his voice low and soothing. "It's just me."

Sagging in relief as she recognized Jason's

voice, Lindsey closed her eyes and swallowed rapidly. With a groan, she threw back the covers and swung her legs over the side of the bed. On legs that felt like they were about to collapse beneath her, she raced to the bathroom. Her stomach heaved, emptying its contents and continuing to spasm until her body ached.

Forcing her shivering body off the cold bathroom floor, she went to the sink, carefully avoiding her reflection in the mirror, and rinsed her mouth. She splashed water over her face and winced at the contact with her cheek where Dominic had cut her. No doubt she would sport an impressive bruise for days and would face another round of uncomfortable questions and looks of pity or contempt. She deserved no pity, and she already held herself in contempt.

She opened the bathroom door and came face to face with Jason. Tension radiated from him as he stood there with his shoulders hunched and his hands shoved deep into the front pockets of his jeans. Concern and questions lit his blue-grey eyes. A tremor wracked Lindsey's body, and she wondered what Jason saw when he looked at her. He pulled his hands out of his pockets and held them out to her, offering an embrace.

With a staggered step, Lindsey closed the

distance between them. Crashing into him, she hid her face against his chest. He carefully wrapped his arms around her.

"Are you all right?" His chest reverberated with the question, making it more felt than heard.

Lindsey's chin quivered and her jaw ached as she ground her teeth. *I killed someone.* Even in her mind, the words sounded shrill and panicked. She tried to shy away from the thought, tried to deny the reality, but the knowledge echoed in her consciousness. *I killed Dominic.*

Jason stroked her hair. "Stupid question." He rested his cheek on top of her head. "Of course you're not."

Lindsey moved her arms around his back and squeezed him to her as the first sob escaped her. He tightened his hold on her. When she quieted, she relaxed her desperate grip. "I'm sorry," she said around a hiccupping breath, her voice muffled against his chest. "I've got your shirt all wet."

"And probably snotty. I'll live."

A tremulous smile tried to form but threatened to turn into another bout of tears.

"Nathan?" Jason asked in a deep murmur.

Lindsey drew a ragged breath. "I got him out. I think he'll be okay."

Jason squeezed her gently. "Do you want to tell me about it?"

Needing no time to consider her answer, Lindsey shook her head.

"If you change your mind..."

"I know. Thank you." Lindsey stayed in Jason's embrace, soaking in his strength and warmth, taking comfort in his presence, until a question occurred to her. Pulling back enough to look up at him, she asked, "Why are you here?"

His gaze drifted to her bruised cheek. Raising a hand, he skimmed his fingertips over it. Lindsey shied from the light contact. He frowned and a slight crease formed between his brows. "Makayla. You left your cell in her car. She called me with it." His slight grin when he met Lindsey's questioning gaze confirmed that he would not have answered if he had known it was Makayla. The grin disappeared, replaced by a somber expression. "She told me about Nathan and what you planned to do." Placing a hand on the back of her head, he pulled her back to his chest. He spoke next to her ear, his voice gruff. "Lindsey, did you think about what could happen to you? What if you had been hurt like Nathan? Who would have saved you?"

Lindsey stiffened. "I had to."

"I know." Jason's fingers combed through her hair. The gentle pull soothed her, and she settled against him. "I know. It's just, when I got here, you were asleep, and I realized I had no idea how to tell if you were in trouble or not. And if I had woken you up, you would've killed me." Lindsey flinched at his choice of expression. "All I could do was watch and wait and hope that you would be all right." Jason's voice grew softer. "If I had lost you…" He sighed. "I love you, Lindsey."

Lindsey closed her eyes against his words, uncertain if he had meant her to hear them. She wished she had not, because she could no longer deny that his feelings for her ran in a different direction than hers for him. Later, she would have to put some distance between them, but for now, although she knew it was selfish, she remained in his embrace, taking the comfort and support he offered.

CHAPTER TWENTY-SIX

"TIME."

Lindsey lowered her pen and looked at her half-finished exam in disgust. It would be a miracle if she passed. She hoped her previous scores were high enough to buoy this one and keep her from failing.

After turning in her paper, Lindsey climbed the stairs and exited the auditorium. On a bench directly opposite the auditorium's double doors, she saw a young man, sitting hunched forward with his elbows resting on his knees and his head bent low. Recognition hit her before he raised his head and she met his impossibly blue eyes. Her breath caught and her heart raced. The other students became background noise as all of her attention focused on Nathan.

Unable to look away, frozen in place more effectively than anything Dominic had managed, Lindsey watched as Nathan slowly got to his feet. Someone bumped into her from behind and propelled her forward. Without thought or hesitation, she walked into Nathan, wrapping her arms around him and burying her face against his chest as his arms went around her.

Lindsey relaxed into the warm, solid feel of him. She turned her head and put her ear over the comforting sound of his heart. Whatever blood stained her, at least this good had come from it—Nathan lived. Some of the tension that had plagued her over the last few weeks eased.

He tightened his hold. Raising his hand, he ran his fingers into her hair. With his hand cupped over her ear, he held her to him. His chin brushed her forehead. When he spoke, his voice seemed to rumble through him. "Lindsey."

She allowed herself to luxuriate in his embrace, but then she loosened her hold and stepped back. The pair stared at each other. His eyes were clouded with emotion. Her gaze lowered to his chest, and the memory of the knife protruding from him, his blood seeping around it, superimposed itself in her vision. She closed her eyes to banish the image. When she felt more in control of the raging emotions within her, she looked to Nathan again. Naked concern shaped his face.

"You're done for the day?" He tipped his head toward the exit.

She nodded and zipped up her jacket. At the door, he reached around her and opened it. They walked side by side through the campus.

"Thank you, Lindsey," Nathan said once they had cleared the press of students.

"You're okay?" She glanced at him, trying to assess his well-being.

"For the most part. I'm still sore, but I'm done with the meds." His features softened as he looked at her. "They tell me I'm lucky."

Lindsey averted her eyes. She thrust her hands deep into her pockets and let her feet carry her across the familiar pathways out of habit.

"You didn't come see me in the hospital."

"I'm not family. I didn't think they'd let me in to see you." She offered the lie in a flat tone.

"You haven't returned my calls."

From the corner of her eye she studied him. "How did you know I was here?"

With a heavy sigh, he lowered his head and shook it before tipping it back and rolling his shoulders. He squinted into the bright noonday sun. "I called Jason," he said in a clipped tone.

Lindsey's steps faltered at his admission, and she looked down at her feet. "Oh." The path forked. Taking the right path put her closer to Nathan, their elbows nearly touching. He followed her lead and made no attempt to put more distance between them.

"So, are you going to talk to me?" he asked. "Or are you going to run away and hide?"

With a sharp intake of breath and wide eyes, Lindsey halted while Nathan continued walking. Hot tears burned her eyes and blurred her vision. Her hands bunched the fabric of her coat pockets.

Like always. He might not have said it, but she heard it in his voice. Would she run and hide like always. The accusation stung. Was he right about her avoiding confrontation? Yes. But, when it mattered most, for his sake, what she had done...Hysterical laughter bubbled up in her throat. She hastily withdrew a hand and slapped it over her mouth.

"Lindsey?"

Her head snapped up. She fixed him with a gaze that concealed nothing but laid bare her anger and pain. Tears coursed down her cheeks, cooling rapidly in the winter air. He reached for her, the remorse plain on his face, but she shuffled back and put up a hand to stop him.

"The only reason you are alive is that I did not run." Emotion choked her voice, made the words come out in a hoarse whisper.

"I kn—"

"No. You want me to talk to you. Fine. I'll talk. You listen." Trembling, she moved closer and pitched her voice low. "You want to know why I didn't come see you in the hospital. I couldn't handle it. I couldn't handle seeing you being treated for the same kind of wound that I inflicted on Dominic. Only, despite being on a ventilator and always having people nearby, Dominic didn't survive. I made sure of that." She tapped her chest with a shaking hand. "I put a knife in his chest and held it there. I held him there. I killed him." Lindsey choked on a sob. "And he *thanked* me."

She turned away from Nathan's stunned expression, sniffed, and drew in a deep, shuddering breath. "You want to know why I haven't returned your calls." Lindsey looked at Nathan and saw his barely contained despair.

"I love you. God help me, I love you. Despite everything, I love you. But," she added, quelling the hope and relief that started to shine in his eyes, "I don't trust you. I can't trust you." He closed his eyes against her words. "And I don't trust myself with you."

When Nathan finally opened his eyes, Lindsey was unable to meet them. The pain she saw there echoed her own. It pulled at her and urged her to offer him comfort. She squelched the impulse, hating the part of her that responded to him. Raw and weary, intending to go home, she stepped to his side. A light, tentative touch on her wrist made her pause.

"Wait. Please. I'm sorry."

"Me too." The words sounded as hollow as she felt. "Goodbye, Nathan."

About the Author

C. E. Czerniejewski is a fan of all things science fiction and fantasy, loves Japanese anime and manga nearly to the point of it being an obsession that includes attending conventions, cosplaying, and collecting more merchandise than is economically wise, and lives in North Carolina among family, friends, and a trio of felines.